AF256976

Christmas Cracker
Copyright©2013 Barry Lowe and Jazmin Starr
ISBN 978-1-909934-39-9
Cover art and design by Dawné Dominique

Published by
Lydian Press 2013
Find us on the World Wide Web at
www.lydianpress.com

CHRISTMAS CRACKER

GAY EROTICA FOR THE HOLIDAYS

Barry Lowe & Jazmin Starr

Lydian Press

CONTENTS

All originally published as individual eBooks by loveyoudivine Alterotica

FIFTY SHADES OF FEY

Barry Lowe

Rudolph's nose isn't the only thing that's red

Screw Rudi. Santa's little helper. Santa's little toy boy more like. "Ooooh, Rudi with your nose so bright pull my sleigh tonight. Take January off because you'll need the rest after all that tiring work." I was noted for my impression of Santa which was so accurate I'd had a lot of fun impersonating him over the PA system at work giving the other elves the day off. The fat old bastard was a slave driver. If people thought the way electronics companies treated their workforce in China was abominable, just let them get a load of the conditions we elves work under making all those Christmas gifts, especially now that modern kids are so greedy and demanding. Long gone are the days when simple but lovingly hand-crafted toys or dolls sufficed, now the little brats want the latest Trojan 5000 game or the latest iThingime or apps that bring the world to them instead of going out and finding it themselves.

No wonder there's so much waste. People don't appreciate shit if they don't have to work for it. I made the mistake of telling him that once. Hoo, boy. You would have thought I'd questioned his whole reason for being. Well, okay, maybe I was. He had been looking a bit frayed around the edges. His red coloring was fading, except for that nose of his with the broken capillaries, but that had more to do with his intake of gin than people's beliefs in his existence.

Wouldn't you know it, just as demand was slacking off enough to make life less of a grind, less miserable for us workers, suddenly the newly prosperous China and other countries jumped on the bandwagon and decided conspicuous consumption was for them, too. Now we're even busier than before. Old Nick instituted new working hours, graveyard shifts, shortened lunch breaks, a week's less vacation a year. Sickness benefits were a thing of the past.

I made the mistake of trying to organize the labor force. Bring in a union. That was about as popular as the sole sex worker on an oil rig platform going down with herpes. And Old Nick looked at me as if I was some sort of terrible disease when he carpeted me in his office.

"I'm soooo disappointed in you, Bardolph," the bastard wheezed, spreading the word 'so' into the longest syllable in the entire history of the world. Please,

God, let one of those unmanned missiles the Americans use on their spy drones shoot the nasty bugger out of the sky on Christmas Day. "Why can't you be more like your twin?"

Okay, my response wasn't the wisest in the world, I admit that now. "Because he's a brown-nose ass-kissing 'look-at-me-I'm-the-favorite' who has his tongue so far up your fat old ass you might as well use him as a suppository."

Even I heard the gasp from the office elves who had their pointy ears pasted to the door listening to my dressing down.

Nick chose to ignore my abuse, instead turning his spleen on my looks and personal habits.

"Look at you," he said slapping me in the stomach. "You're getting fat."

That was rich coming from someone who would be categorized as clinically obese in the 'real' world. What a role model to give kids, eh? He couldn't even do up the zipper on his frayed red coat anymore. It hardly covered his burgeoning belly, and his poor neglected wife had run out of material to let the garment out. The old coat was such a patchwork of patches and gussets it was in danger of splitting apart every time he wore it, which he only did now on ceremonial occasions. All other times he wore a T-shirt and shorts. Eww, so not a good look.

"Perhaps you're not working out hard enough. Don't I supply all you elves with a gymnasium to keep your bodies in trim? Don't I feed you well?"

"I'm so buggered after my regular shift at the factory, Nick, all I can do is drag my poor exhausted body back to my dorm for sleep. Then it's up at sparrow's fart to do it all over again. As for the food, yeah, um, burgers and fries are nice and I know how much you love them, but I think you need a qualified nutritionist to help vary the canteen meals and maybe introduce a few vegetables other than the deep-fried potato."

"Never did me any harm," he gloated, letting go with a serious fart that echoed around the room, just before the top button of his shorts finally gave up the struggle, flying past my ear to ping against the far wall before expiring on the carpet. So much for superiority.

I thought the eloquence of the displaced button made any further comment from me superfluous.

"What am I going to do with you?" he asked as he paced the office.

It was a rhetorical question. He wasn't asking my opinion because he would have already made up his mind what punishment was my due. The United Nations talks a lot about Democracy but what we have here is a dictatorship. Nick's an immortal so there's no chance we'll ever be ruled by anyone more benevolent, or that we'll ever get to vote on anything. Hell, we make the

Vatican and the Dalai Lama look positively benign politically in comparison.

Nick may have believed that his punishment fitted the crime; I found it harsh and unnecessary. Perhaps not unnecessary – someone had to do it. But it was a shit job usually reserved for the intransigent, the criminal or the insane. To give the old miser credit, he was slowly implementing new technology but some areas were still in the grip of the old-fashioned meters which required on-site readings, much like the gas and electricity meters of yore. Most of the world was now hooked up to Santa's mainframe computer that automatically registered each and every human's naughty or nice quotient until, at midnight on December 24, it spat out a list of those who were deemed worthy of Santa's largesse.

I pulled my thin coat tighter around my body, fluffed up my wet scarf around my mouth and nose to prevent the cold from penetrating, and yanked my colorful beanie down over my head to protect the pointy tips of my ears. Sighing loudly, I put my head down to strike out against the buffeting flurry of snow.

Why the fuck couldn't he have sent me somewhere warm, like Australia?

I knew why. This was punishment. Only the worst suburb in the worst city in the world was good enough for me. While my older brother, Rudolph, sat back home in centrally heated comfort sipping his cinnamon-flavored heated red wine in preparation for the wearying Christmas haul, I put my head down to butt against the snow and wind that stung my face, making the fine hairs bristle on my chin. I cursed again, knowing that by the time I got back having sent my readings electronically – if only I could transport my body in such a fashion – I'd be so buggered that when the alarm went off the following morning I'd have so much difficulty shifting, Nick would whip me to hurry along my transformation.

Mean old tosser. Not only do we work back-breaking shifts to manufacture the commodities of Christmas, and live in absolute squalor, a 'chosen' bunch of us are also expected to pull the bloody sleigh as Santa distributes his largesse. It's always been the way. The CEO garners all the praise for goods made on the sweat of the common worker elf. What made it doubly galling for me was that my more successful brother was always head of the pack because of his bloody nose. Shiny, my ass. It was riddled with broken capillaries from all the alcohol he tossed down his throat as Santa's drinking companion. That's what made it glow the first time. He's nothing special. Just an ordinary everyday drunk who lights up from too much booze on Christmas Eve.

By the time we return from deliveries, he's so sozzled with alcohol-laced Christmas cake and other goodies that Santa feeds him he's useless baggage. Just as well the sleigh's empty on the return bout otherwise his dead weight would pull us down over the North Atlantic. Selfish bastard.

I consulted my clipboard to see how many houses to go. That was the joy of apartment buildings. You could stand in the comparative shelter and warmth of the basement while you scanned meter information onto the special phones we carried. Houses were different. No new-fangled technology for them, everything had to be laboriously entered on the clipboard and then entered manually on the phone once I'd found a café or burger joint that had free Wi-Fi. Didn't I tell you how stingy…oh, forget it.

One house left. Number 18. I stood in front of it. And shuddered.

Oh, fuck!

How could I possibly forget Number 18 Cherrybrook Lane. The address sounded so innocuous but any number of elves had attempted to read the Naughty or Nice Meter but had returned empty-handed and seriously psychologically battered and physically bruised, refusing to answer questions as to what had occurred. I'd heard rumors but they'd obviously been exaggerated out of all reality and were fantastically absurd, some of them about underground Mole Men who ate elves for breakfast, others about a tribe of naked hairy Neanderthals whose pagan rituals included torture and dismemberment. I didn't believe them for a moment.

However, I knew whatever the reality it would not be pleasant. Someone back at HQ had set me up to fail. Not only fail, but return battered and brutalized so I could cause no more disruption to the smooth running of Santa's dictatorship. I was tempted to turn around and go back the way I came, smearing a little dirt on my face, making a few tears in my clothes, perhaps smacking my arm against a concrete block enough to bruise it (my arm not the concrete) in an effort to convince that I had at least tried.

Nah, they'd see through me.

I marched right past the house and on to the nearest fast food outlet where I sent off the final collations. If something happened to me I didn't want anyone else to suffer because I hadn't sent in the correct forms for the final houses in the street. My work done, and my hunger slaked with a burger, fries and a fizzy soda, I headed back to my last task. The two-story mansion at Number 18 had an eerie familiarity, as if it were the understudy for the creepy house on the hill in *Psycho*.

From the pavement, the building appeared dark and forlorn as if napping, just waiting for someone to stray onto its vast network of manicured lawns, ready to spring at the slightest trespass. It was late afternoon and the gables and eaves cast eerie shadows over the property. I suspect it was my imagination that did the rest but I was certainly uneasy as I opened the gate quietly and ducked behind a clump of bushes to one side of the front garden. I was hidden both from the street and the house itself. It was unusual to enter by the front entrance in such an audacious manner because if anyone had been watching they would have seen me duck behind cover.

Usually we gained entrance via the back of a property but I knew in this case it backed onto another yard which would have meant twice the opportunity to be seen. I reckoned that my brazen approach was the best. I remained hidden to see if anyone called me on my behavior. When, after fifteen minutes, no one had appeared and the house slumbered undisturbed, I kept low as the shadows grew longer, much like thick dark hands stretching out to meet me, striding toward the side of the house.

No inside lights were illuminated so I assumed I was pretty safe when I found the small basement window and jimmied it open. It wasn't difficult and I marveled that the security on such a grand residence was so slack. Of course, the whole place could be wired to a security firm which meant a squad car would pull up shortly. I only breathed easier when ten minutes passed and there was no sign of the cops or a security company.

This was almost too easy. That should have set off warning bells in my mind. I guess I was tired, a little pissed, a lot chagrined at having been assigned the shit task, so my brain was not focusing on the task at hand. Naturally, I began to squeeze through the window and wouldn't you know it, I got stuck fast. Bloody Santa was right, I'd put on weight. I made my New Year's Resolution there and then: portion control and at least three days a week at the gym.

I had no intention of keeping to it but by sending the message out into the ether that I was serious I hoped something might save me. Something did, although not in the manner I expected. I wriggled my body from side to side in a futile effort to dislodge myself, my legs dangling into the basement, most of my torso and my head in the side yard.

Hearing footsteps approach, I wriggled more determinedly. If I was discovered I was in deep shit. It was a bit like being a spy during the war; I could give my name and rank and serial number but no further details. I was never ever allowed to give out information about the Naughty or Nice Meters – on pain of execution. Maybe that's an exaggeration. On pain of banishment. A few elves had been banished in my time, including friends of mine. I never heard from them again. Fortunately for the Old Fat Bastard, it seems the information gleaned from the torture of elves was either disbelieved or of no import for we never received unwelcome visitors in all the years we'd been tucked away in…there, I almost blew it. You won't get me that easily.

I could hear panting as the footsteps came closer. Obviously someone was out of condition. There didn't seem much chance I would be able to free myself so I was preparing to call for help resigning myself to punishment. A number of scenarios went through my mind: I lost my football and was attempting to retrieve it, I slipped and fell through the basement window…each excuse became more and more ridiculous.

Oh, no. The footsteps came around the side of the house.

"Stop it. Stop it at once," I begged as the large Labrador retriever licked my face. I was grateful he was at least friendly and his tail was wagging excitedly but his licks were tickling me and his slobber was getting in my eyes. That was unfortunate because it meant I couldn't see who the voice belonged to when I heard him mutter, "Well, well. What do we have here?"

My wrists were gripped strongly and my body was tugged hard; all to no avail.

"Looks like you could stand to lose a little weight if you're gonna go around breaking into people's properties," he chuckled.

"My weight is none of your business," I huffed, attempting to look up at the man whose worn leather boots I was restricted to ogling. I couldn't raise my head higher than his crotch which seemed to be packed with all sorts of delicious goodies.

"Well, lad, it is my business if you're gonna be stuck fast in my basement window over the Christmas New

Year period. It can get mighty cold around here at night and if you freeze to death it'll make it even more difficult to remove you."

As if to reinforce what he said, it began to snow again.

"I think I'm in more danger of being slobbered to death," I replied sarcastically.

The dog obviously didn't like my tone because he lifted his leg directly in front of my face. I groaned and closed my eyes and mouth tightly.

"No, Racer."

I wasn't sure the command would do any good at that late stage but the dog's owner had shoved him out of the way and he pissed all over the side wall a few feet from my predicament.

"Thanks," I said. "Although it might have warmed me up."

The guy laughed. "Hang on, I'll go inside and see if I can pull you out of the window by your feet."

"Take Racer with you. Please," I pleaded.

I didn't know how much more doggy affection I could take.

"Come on, Racer."

I was in real trouble. I struggled to get free hoping I could unwedge myself and escape before the home owner could get to the basement and prevent me leaving. It was a much lesser sin to return without a meter reading than it was to be caught. Failing that, I suppose I could offer to help relieve the constriction in his crotch. Not likely he was gay, but I could dream.

It was no use. Struggling just seemed to make my predicament worse and the window frame was beginning to feel like razor blades slicing into my belly. There'd be marks for sure. I moved in an attempt to redistribute my weight, but to no avail.

Feeling a tug at my ankles, I realized the owner was inside. He pulled gently for which I was thankful and although I moved a little, my clothing got caught on the wooden window frame, holding me tight.

"I think I can see the problem," the muffled voice said. "I'll have you out in no time."

Being freed would be just the beginning of my problems; especially if he called the police. Perhaps he already had.

I felt my boots being unlaced and pulled from my feet. He at least left my socks on.

"Can you unfasten your coat and shirt? I think that's what's jamming you in the window. Can you take them off, then I can yank you through quickly before you freeze?"

Fortunately, my hands were free so I attempted to follow his instructions, managing it with some difficulty. However, I stopped when I felt him fumble with the belt to my trousers. What was he playing at?

"Come on, help me out," he shouted. "I haven't got all day."

Suddenly the lower half of my body felt cold. My trousers had been whipped off and, if my senses weren't playing me false, my undies with them. No, my senses were spot on. I knew because I felt a large masculine hand stroke my butt before slapping down hard on both cheeks.

"Nice," he said as I shouted more at the indignity than the pain.

I worked more quickly at getting my coat and shirt off before he could slap me about any further.

"Ready," I said. "Hurry, it's bloody freezing out here."

I couldn't remove my clothes altogether but if I held my hands above my head as he pulled they'd be scraped off by the tightness of the frame.

"Let all your breath out and after three…one, two, three…"

I was about to complain when I felt his hands grasp my ankles and in no time my body was forcibly drawn through the wooden mouth to the basement. I yelled as the skin on my stomach and my back scraped against the rough timber, I managed to turn my head at the last moment so it squeezed through the small opening without more injury than a bump to my chin. Then I was falling.

"Gotcha," he said, catching me in his arms. "My, aren't you the pretty one?"

My eyes were watering from the chaffed skin but his comment made me look up. His arms were powerful, rippling with muscle that was scarcely concealed by his tight shirt. But what totally disarmed me was his face. He has a full beard, neatly trimmed, a broad brow, the cutest nose that had obviously been broken somewhere in the past and had never set one hundred per cent correctly giving it an appealing detour, but, above all, were his hazel eyes that seems to shift from brown through grey to green. I could paddle in those eyes.

He looked at me as if expecting an answer to his unspoken question. I had no idea what excuse I could offer that wouldn't sound ridiculous. If only I could keep my identity secret. Mind you, it's difficult to disguise who we are; our pointed ears are a dead giveaway.

I felt so comfortable in his arms that I would have been happy to remain there all day, until I realized I was totally naked except for my socks, my cock giving away my excitement.

"Not only pretty, but you're a big boy as well," he said, lowering me to the floor.

It was warm in the basement so I hadn't noticed my nudity but now I grabbed for my trousers.

"I don't think so," my captor said, wrenching them out of my hands. "But I will go and retrieve your shirt and coat from outside. If you know what's good for you, you won't try to escape."

So saying he slammed the window closed before heading for the cellar door, taking my clothes with him.

"Make yourself at home," he laughed as he disappeared, locking the exit behind him.

That's when I noticed the basement was all set up like a dungeon with tools of torment and torture adorning the walls. Shit, out of the frying pan into the fire. Of all the rotten luck.

I tried the door but, as expected, there was no way I could escape via that means before he returned.

Fascinated by all the paraphernalia on the walls, I examined it more closely. There were various paddles and floggers, plus some rather nasty looking crocodile clips which I realized were tit or scrotum clamps. I shuddered as I imagined the teeth biting into my flesh. There were padded cuffs, manacles, chains and ropes, spreader bars, and a cross. I wasn't totally ignorant; I knew that these implements weren't the props for a passion play. This was serious kink, which was confirmed when I discovered a secret cache of dildos and butt plugs.

However, it was the sling hanging from the wooden beams in the ceiling that fascinated me. It drew me forward until I was unselfconsciously stroking the leather seat wondering what it would be like…I had to shake my head to break the spell.

Although attracted by what I'd discovered, I needed to get out of there. This place was full-on and though I'd flirted with this subculture in the past it had been only in the safety of my fantasies. My captor slapping my ass had awakened something inside me but I wasn't sure the pain was worth exploring, especially not after examining the rather lethal looking objects on the wall.

But the sling. Its siren call was so hypnotic. As if in a trance, I kept returning to it, until I could ignore its lure no longer. I wanted to try it just once. Needed to try it. I hoisted myself up into it, almost falling out as it swung precariously because of my inexperience. As I lay back and the surge of seasickness abated, I felt so comfortable exhaustion overwhelmed me and I fell asleep.

The swat against my ass woke me. I was disoriented by the shock of the sting in my butt, the unfamiliar surroundings, and the fact my wrists were constrained above my head in cuffs and my ankles were also cuffed and raised in the air giving anyone free access to my ass. Another smack and I was fully awake.

"Cut it out!" I snapped.

"If it's something I can't stand, it's someone who can't take his punishment like a man."

The voice was deep and resonated in my balls. My cock, which had obviously been asleep along with the rest of my body, perked up in interest. Now that I looked at him more closely, more was revealed of my jailer. The fact he was almost naked had something to do with the revelation. He wore a leather harness and leather shorts but little else. I couldn't move my body sufficiently to see his legs but I suspected he was wearing leather boots. He was quite the package. I could imagine plenty of gay men wanting to wake up to this daddy in their Christmas stocking. The incredibly handsome bearded face was the least of his charms. His solid muscular body sported a chest covered in fine fur that spread like prairie grass down over his belly finally disappearing under the band of his shorts.

He was a sight I'd be glad to wake up to every morning.

He swatted me again.

"What were you doing breaking into my house?"

"I wasn't breaking in," I corrected.

"What, you'd already broken in and were trying to escape when you got wedged in the window? You put on weight while you were inside my home?"

"You sure are a sarcastic bastard," I said before I thought through my response.

That earned me another whack with the paddle. Too close to my balls for comfort.

"Cut that out!" I snapped.

"I don't think you're in any position to tell me what to do," he grinned. "Besides, every time I tan your ass, your cock leaks."

"That's because it doesn't know what's good for it."

"Oh, I think it does. It knows better than you do."

He picked up a riding crop and ran it along the underside of my very hard prick before flicking it against the shaft. I hissed.

"Now answer the question."

I remained mum. This time he struck twice. Okay, so it stung, but I thought my cock was going to explode with the pleasure. That was weird.

"Look," I said in an attempt to prevent another blow. "I had no intention of robbing you."

"Yeah, right," he said. "What is it with you guys? Every year around this time, I find one of you trying to break in or else inside trying to get out. Are you all related or something?"

"In a way," I admitted.

"Big family," he snickered. "This has been going on ever since I moved in fifteen years ago.

I did a quick calculation. That would make him in his early forties. Yum. Just the age I like my daddies.

"You're definitely the cutest of the lot," he added.

My cock did its best not to crow at the praise, but failed miserably and allowed a drool of pre-cum to spill onto my stomach.

"You like that, eh?" he said, gripping my cock in his hand, stroking it a number of times.

"Please," I begged, hoping he'd take pity of me and end my torment. "Please."

"Please what?" he asked.

Oh, come on, he wasn't serious.

"Sir?"

"Good boy," he praised, jerking my cock a few times. "You learn fast."

Not fast enough, it seems, for he grabbed my balls and squeezed hard, a lightning bolt of pain shooting through my groin.

"Okay, boy. What were you doing breaking into my house?"

"I wasn't."

He squeezed my balls tighter.

There was no lie that would make any sense. Problem was, the truth sounded even more outrageous.

As the silence lengthened, he put more pressure on my testicles until I thought they'd pop like a bloated pimple. I struggled in the sling, arching my back, anything to get away from the pressure.

"Okay, okay," I screamed. "I'll tell you the truth, just release my balls."

He did. "The truth, mind you," he instructed, flicking the end of the crop against my ball sack for emphasis. I shuddered at the damage he might be inclined to inflict on me.

I sighed loudly. Banishment would have to be better than crushed testes.

I must have taken too long to collect my thoughts because he tapped my scrotum again as a reminder.

"Okay, give me time to get my thoughts in order," I said.

"You shouldn't need time if it's the truth," he warned.

I spoke more sharply than I intended, given my precarious situation. "Look, the truth is so much more bizarre than you realize and revealing it puts my whole future at stake, so give me a bit of leeway here, okay?"

"Feisty little thing, aren't you?"

"Enough of the little. I'm big for my background."

"What are you? Five six?"

"Yeah."

"Height not big in your family?"

"Average is around five four," I said. "I'm considered tall."

I looked at my captor who was around six foot. Mmm, very nice.

I wish my brain would stop doing that.

He taped my cock. "And well hung."

I didn't have much choice but to tell the truth although I'd leave out as much as I could. Maybe I'd only get a partial banishment.

"I'm listening," he said.

"Here. Lift the hair off my ears."

I always wore my hair long because it covered the tell-tale signs of elfish. He brushed my hair aside, pushing it behind my ear. He stepped back suddenly.

"Christ. What happened? Thalidomide or some shit like that?"

I was offended by his reaction because I prided myself on the beauty of my ears. They tapered to a slim conical peak, the most sensitive area on an elf's body. In fact, sometimes my ears stimulated me more than my cock.

"They're perfectly natural, Philistine."

"You're telling me you're an alien of some sort?"

"Not exactly."

"Then what exactly are you saying?" He tapped the riding crop against my nipples as a warning.

"I'm not from outer space, if that's what you mean."

"Then what are you?"

"I'm an elf."

He guffawed but not before he'd slapped my left nipple with a force that went straight to my cock. "A fuckin' elf. Don't tell me, you and your mob come around near Christmas each year to see if I've been naughty or nice, is that it?"

I thought he understood although the tone of his voice should have told me otherwise. "Exactly."

My right nipple copped a hiding.

"Okay," I moaned. "I told you that you wouldn't believe me."

"You're not wrong, boy."

I had no option. "Over in the corner." I gave him instructions where to look. It was with a great deal of skepticism, and not a little humor, he removed some of his sex toys to discover the meter.

"What is that?"

"It's a Naughty or Nice Meter."

"You've got quite an imagination, lad. But telling porkies won't save your ass."

I tried a new tack. "Who says I want to save my ass?"

That pulled him up in his tracks. He smiled, unzipping his shorts and kicking them off.

"This promises to be a very merry Christmas, indeed."

I might get out of my predicament yet.

He pulled my head toward his prick which was thick and semi-tumescent. I wasn't sure I'd be able to take it all but I'd give it a bloody good try. I'd never sucked a human before. As soon as he pushed it between my lips I knew I was addicted. Elf cock is fine but there was something extra special about this cock. Maybe I was falling in love.

Before I took it into my gob fully, I asked, "What's your name?"

"Stefan," he said. "What's yours?"

"Bardolph."

"Unusual. Eastern European?"

"Elf."

That did it. He shoved his cock to the back of my mouth, instructing me to suck it. He added, "You can call me Sir."

I liked his name but I also liked the fact he wanted to dominate me. Elves are a fuckin' miserable lot. We're so used to servitude because Nick is the only Dom in town. He doesn't like competition, so we elves playact at being Doms and we're bloody awful at it. I think so anyway. Now I had a forty carat human Dom shoving his cock into my throat and I couldn't believe my luck. What had begun as a shit job that was little more than punishment had morphed into punishment that was little short of Elfin heaven.

As Sir's cock expanded to its full thickness, I opened my throat to accept him.

"Shit, boy, you really know how to please a man."

That was praise indeed. I redoubled my efforts until I heard a sharp intake of breath and Sir tugged my head away from his prick. I'd tasted the salty pre-cum from the slit hoping he'd gift me with his load.

"Not yet, boy," he said, stroking my ears, "I want to feel your ass around my cock before I dump my first load."

First? If I believed in angels, they'd be singing now.

Sir ran his finger down the crack of my ass until he reached my tight puckered hole. I shivered in anticipation. He pushed and I opened as best I could but it had been so long that his finger could not penetrate far.

"You're so tight. Daddy is gonna love breaching that ass of yours. Tell me you want it, boy."

I knew how to beg because elves were good at it in role play. This time, however, I really meant it. "Please, Sir, fuck my ass. I want your cock inside me so bad."

"I do believe you do, boy," he smiled. "And who am I to refuse such an honest request."

He grabbed a jar and began to lube my ass lips, pressing his index finger in slowly to loosen me up. I moaned at the intrusion wanting to feel more than a finger inside me.

"Your ass is so hot and tight," he whispered. He was as turned on as I was.

"I saved it for you, Sir."

He probed a second finger inside me, manipulating them to lube me inside as well as out. My ass cunt gripped them tightly.

"That's it, squeeze, boy. I never felt anyone who could tighten their boy pussy like you can. I don't think I can wait any more to feel it grip my cock."

He slathered grease on his prick before aiming it at my hole. The head pushed inside without regard for my comfort. I balled my hands into fists and struggled to get away from the penetration.

"Keep still, boy. The burn will go away shortly."

I relaxed and sure enough his cock felt just right in my ass. He sensed my acquiescence and began the process of embedding his human cock as deep as he could. As he sank deeper inside me, his cock brushed against my prostate and I cried out in pleasure.

"You like that?" he asked.

I nodded my head, unable to speak because my body throbbed with so much pleasure.

I looked into his eyes. He was watching me and I thought I could see a genuine concern for my welfare.

"You're so beautiful, boy," he whispered. "I don't know what Fates brought you to my house but I would very much like to thank them. I don't know if I'm gonna be able to let you go."

My mouth engaged before my brain. "Then don't."

Did I really say that?

He pushed his cock all the way inside me, gasping as his balls came to rest against my ass.

"So hot, boy. Your ass is on fire."

I squeezed his prick with my sphincter to encourage him to start plowing my butt.

"Fuck me hard, Sir. Make me yours. Mark me," I whimpered.

"Oh, God. What did I do to deserve you?"

The feeling was quite mutual.

He began ramming his cock into my guts, plowing me like he couldn't get enough of me then easing off as he obviously came close to blowing his load.

"I could keep this up for days," he admitted.

"Why don't you?" I asked.

"You got anywhere you need to be?"

Did I? Back with the Fat Old Bastard where I'd be hauled over the coals for my failure, demoted at the very least, banished at the very most. Shit, I might just as well stay here and take my chances.

"Yes, Sir," I replied.

His look of disappointment confirmed what I suspected. It also made my decision easier.

"I need to be here with you, Sir," I added.

He smiled. "I can arrange that, boy."

He pounded my ass harder, almost as if he wanted his entire body inside me.

"Sir, please suck the points of my ears."

He looked slightly perturbed but I increased the spasms of my ass around his cock to drive him wild and he leaned over to lick my ear lobe, working his way tentatively to the tip before taking it in his mouth and sucking.

My entire body bucked with the charge that raced through my body. I pushed my ass back against his penetrating cock until I thought I'd burst. Sir panted like he'd never felt anything like it before.

"Oh my God," he screamed. "I'm gonna come."

"Suck my ear," I screamed.

He plowed into me while sucking my ear like it was my prick. I went first, my cock pulsing as I shot so much spunk between our bodies I thought we'd both drown.

The spasms must have set him off because a few moments later I felt him flood my guts with his own jizz tsunami.

He slumped over my body, exhausted from the effort.

Supported by the leather sling, I lay back wanting more than anything to put my arms around him, to cuddle him close.

"That was the best ever, boy," he puffed. "You keep that up, I may never let you go."

Should I tell him I react really well to threats?

OMG!
SANTA'S GOT A SIX-PACK!

Barry Lowe

Not all Santas are fat, old bastards.

"I've been watching you. You're really wonderful with children."

Holy Bat toast with Robin jam, Mr. Perfect is talking to me!

I snapped my lips together knowing that if I opened my mouth I would make a total fool of myself. See above reaction. My mouth always engaged before my brain even woke up to what it was saying. 'Juvenile' is the word most of my boyfriends used to describe my childish reaction to everything around me. I say boyfriends but most of them didn't hang around longer than the two-and-a-half minutes it took them to blow up my ass.

Those that did last longer usually ended up braying, "When are you gonna grow up?" before making their exit, inevitably after a break-up fuck.

But it's not me you want to read about, is it? If I'd called the story of my life Santa's got a Skinny Butt, you wouldn't even have put it on your Wish List let alone bought it. So let's get to the selling point: Mr. Perfect. Not his real name. I guess you've already sussed that out for yourself. No one's ever accused me of being the brightest bulb in the chandelier.

He looked very patrician. At least I thought so. I was going to call him Patricia, but that seemed a bit insulting somehow. I settled for Mr. Perfect because he looked like my comic book superhero of the same name. But I'm getting ahead of myself.

You see, me and Thelma have names for all the people who line up with their children. Helps pass the time. Usually it's some tic or habit or facial feature we zone in on and then we give them a moniker like the villains in Dick Tracy. We even had a Pruneface. Not that he looked like a prune in this case, it's just his tone and personality gave us the shits. He was the sort of character who spoke in capital letters.

He attracted our attention by snapping his fingers at us, "You There! My Child Has Been Waiting Absolutely Ages To See Santa. How Long Will It Take?" His attitude got him the animosity of the people in front of him in the line and the sympathy of those behind him, except for Mr. Perfect who gave me a sympathetic smile.

Pruneface's daughter clutched his trousers, trying to hide among the pin-stripes, obviously terrified of meeting the jolly fat man in the red suit, but he'd missed that salient point.

"I Can't Afford To Waste My Time With This Nonsense. I Have Important Meetings To Attend," he added.

Keeping my voice level, although I would have dearly loved to shout at him, I told him, "It's not all about you, sir, it's about the children. If you can't spare the time now, then may I suggest you come back at a time more convenient to yourself when you will be able to wait your turn again."

A few people snickered; a few others gave me what I like to think were grins of appreciation.

See what I mean, though? I can't help myself.

Thelma's the same, but much older. She must be close to a million years old but she says she's closer to fifty-five. I think she's injecting monkey glands because she knows so much stuff, she has to be way older, or else she's somehow transplanted Google into her head instead of a brain.

There I go again. You'd never know I was nineteen and studying to be a graphic artist. Ultimate aim? To rule the universe! I say that but it's not true. I'm not the ruler type. More the set square or compass. *LOL* Maybe not. Real ultimate aim, not fooling around? To draw the best comic book ever. That's the ultimate dream, but I won't be too unhappy if I end up drawing the best comic I can.

It's a bit personal. At the moment, I'm doing it for myself, not for publication. See, I'm just starting out, so it's practice. I showed it to Thel and she said I was 'really talented.' She's just being nice. She did say, though, that Mr. Perfect is not a real good name for a superhero and that if her hubby had been as packed in the underpants department as my cartoon Mr. Perfect she never would've left him. I stopped showing her after that. She knows I'm gay, I'm not ashamed or embarrassed by that, but I was scared she might think I was an unsuitable candidate for this job.

Both Thel and me are elves. Not real elves. All we get to wear is the hat and booties. Green felt rubbish that makes my hair and my feet hot. The real elves get to wear the total green outfit which is even bigger rubbish. But they get more money and have to stay in character all day. They tried me out on that but I was as crap as their costume. They thought my sense of humor was better served looking after the kiddies while they lined up to sit on Santa's knee. Our job is to keep them in line so they don't get too noisy or rambunctious, entertaining them with simple party tricks or jokes while they wait their turn. Parents seem to appreciate it.

So do the Santas. There are a half dozen of them because no one could stand the racket or the unruly behavior for eight hours without a lot of breaks. It's hot and tiring work and sometimes a Santa gets a bit emotional. Or drunk. Then management will dismiss him and find a replacement. A couple of them want me to sit on their laps – when they're naked. I'm polite. It's Mr. Perfect I want sliding down my chimney. Actually, up my chimney.

That's enough background. You're probably eager to get back to Mr. P. who's still waiting for some sort of response from me whose jaw has dropped to the floor in cartoon surprise at being addressed. Without thinking, I bend down to mime picking it up. He looked at me kinda strange.

"What are you doing?" he asked.

"Picking up my jaw," I said.

At least he laughed. "You're a queer one."

"Queer as in 'oddball' or queer as in 'gay'? Or both. And is it a bad thing?"

Yep, I did say it out loud. I squeezed my eyes shut and screwed up my face at my stupidity, waiting for him to call my supervisor to complain.

Mr. P. did not have a chance right then because a young boy tugged at his coat and in a most severe manner as only a six-year-old can, said, "Mister, bugger off, he was telling us a joke and he hasn't finished."

Apologizing profusely to the young audience, Mr. P. backed off, smiling broadly at the reprimand. Just before I got back to the joke which required all my skills mimicking various woodland animals, Mr. P.

whispered, "I liked the way you handled Pruneface. Well done."

I couldn't believe it; he nicknamed him Pruneface as well.

You ever get a buzz so powerful you seem to float through the day? Without drugs, I mean. Everything goes so right it's the moment you want to last forever. Or else, you just want to die then and there because life will never get any better. That moment was mine.

After work, when I got back to my bedsit, it looked like a palace not the cockroach infested dump it really was. The vermin became horses carting me off to the ball where I'd dance with the handsome prince and…

I grabbed my draft paper and my pencils; the work flowing out of me like my body was a conduit to that big library of ideas in the sky. I was so happy, I forgot to eat, almost forgetting to sleep until fatigue overtook me and my head flopped onto my drawing board.

I would have probably remained in that position all night except the knock to my head woke me enough that I staggered to bed. I was so tired I slept in the next morning and was almost late for work. No time for breakfast, I just grabbed my sketches and ran down the stairs. I got through store security and was at my locker with five minutes to spare, enough time to ram the stupid hat on my head so I looked like a stick of asparagus, but not enough to grab a muffin from the canteen.

You might wonder why I'd want a job like this. Well, I actually enjoyed entertaining the kids. They could be little brats, sure, but I identified with their wide-eyed wonder at a world still full of possibilities. Too many of them would grow into the Prunefaces of the future. I hoped I could help just one or two of them avoid that fate. I think the word you're looking for is 'naïve.' Hell, I've been called worse.

The main reason for liking this job is that I don't have to scrub the stink of fried fat off my clothes and my body and out of my hair when I get home at night like I do the other ten months of the year to pay for my tuition and my rent and my paper and ink and pencils. It's great there are fast food outlets that employ young guys like me, dreamers I mean, otherwise I don't know what I'd do.

It's not like my parents would or could help me out financially. I put 'would' first because dad wanted me to work on the roads like him. "Good solid, dependable work, boy," he often told me as I was growing up, there's those words again, floundering about searching for something I wanted to do. "It's not all about you, you know," was his favorite expression. I guess that's why I used it on Pruneface.

Dad would then say something like, "Dreams are all very well in the bedroom late at night, but best to leave them there when you wake up to the real world in the morning. What you need is something dependable. Something that will pay the bills and put the food on the table."

When he said that, I'd think about what was in the fridge: cheap cuts of meat on the turn so they'd inevitably be cut up and disguised in stews, vegetables so flaccid and pock-marked it was a wonder mum could cut enough nutrition from around the spoiled bits to make them worthwhile, and, let's not forget his beer.

Food was a necessary evil to dad. He hated spending money on it. His ill-fitting dentures didn't help the cause of better dietary habits either. Most of his food was mushy because it hurt him to chew. Beer was an entirely different matter. He was praying for the day nutritionists declared it a 'food.' Until then, he had to have the best. Well, why not? You don't have to chew beer.

It wasn't until I left home that I realized what a bang-up job mum did with the little she had. Still, it came as a bit of a shock to discover that food actually had taste, individual tastes, not just some glutinous generic taste of mush.

Oh, hell. I'm rabbiting on about me again, aren't I? Where was I? That's it, almost late for work because… never mind, you've read that bit already. I raced into Santa's Cave to stand beside Thel as security counted down to opening time. There was always an initial rush of parents and offspring, mums and dads not averse to using a bit of elbow power to get to the front of the queue.

Our attempts at crowd control were always short lived. The best we could do was attempt to funnel the enthusiasm, I would have called it the melee if I'd been honest, away from the adult shoppers who were buying exorbitantly expensive decorations, wrapping paper, and the other bib bobs that go with the holiday season, at the counters adjacent to Santa's Cave.

I wasn't going home for Christmas this year. Mum and dad didn't need me freeloading and it's not like we were all that close anyway. Not since they'd found certain drawings of mine which revealed it was as unlikely I'd ever settle down and marry that nice Kylie girl from down the road as it was I'd end up with a job on the roads. As a result there was a minimum of fuss when I declared my intention of moving to the city to study graphic arts for a career in advertising, apart from dad declaring that "No good will come of it, you mark my words," and a slight moistening of the eyes when mum came to see me off at the station.

I sent gifts and received a card from mum with a ten dollar note inside plus instructions to 'buy yourself something nice.' I loved my parents; I just didn't want to be them. So, even though my stomach rumbled its rebellion as I marshaled kids like sheep to the Santa, I was happy. Okay, my bed-sit was crap, I had a lousy paid job, but I still, with pretty strict economizing, had time and a little cash to do what I loved – drawing. And the absolute blue icing on a green cake: I'd met my model for Mr. Perfect which is why I was so bloody tired and hungry right at this moment.

My head rang with the shrieks and screams of young children demanding rewards from Santa for being good for the whole year. It really was the wrong way to go about it. I never believed you should bribe children into good behavior. What did I know? I would never have any of my own.

My stomach gave a volcanic rumble, enough to startle the kids standing near me, bringing to mind the old adage that breakfast is the most important meal of the day, and therefore I should not have been surprised when I could scarcely concentrate on what I was doing. One minute I was turning my hunger grumblings into a creature attempting to claw its way out of my belly to the delight of my young audience as well as the stunned disbelief of some of the more staid parents, the next I was lying on my ass among the plastic bunting that surrounded Santa's Castle, a young worried face hovering over me, asking, "Mister, are you all right?"

Holy Batcrap, I must have fainted.

Parents pulled their children away lest I have some contagious disease before Thel was kneeling beside me, her face a mask of concern. "Are you all right, love?"

I didn't have time to answer before an authoritative voice broke through the confusion. "Stand aside please, I'm a doctor."

"I don't need a doctor," I whined, until I saw who the voice belonged to. Mr. Perfect kneeled beside me, placing the palm of his hand on my forehead. Mmm, maybe I did just need to lie here like Sleeping Beauty waiting for my prince to kiss me better.

"I just didn't have any breakfast," I hissed at him. "I'm fine."

I didn't want to attract an audience as it might mean my job.

"If you're a doctor, where's your scalpel?" one smart little girl asked.

"I can see you're going to be a detective when you grow up," Mr. Perfect smiled at her. "You don't miss anything, do you?"

She beamed at the praise. He leaned into the crowd of children and said in a stage whisper, "I didn't want to scare the patient, but his condition is serious. If I don't operate soon, the monster in his stomach will eat its way out and then we're all doomed."

His audience giggled nervously as Mr. P. swept me up in his arms and carried me toward the staff canteen like a prince carrying off his princess. I knew I would never feel like this again as long as I lived so I breathed in, storing his masculine aroma mixed with soap and a citrus after shave for later fantasies. Surreptitiously, I snuggled against his chest, wondering what mountain they'd carved him from.

Kicking open the canteen door marked STAFF ONLY, he carried me to an empty table and poured me into one of the chairs. He seemed as reluctant to let me go as I was to leave the safety of his brawny arms.

"Sit!" he commanded as the few late morning shift personnel sipping their heart starting beverages of choice stared open mouthed at my superhero striding to the counter to order my breakfast. None of the soggy Bain Marie slush for him. He demanded freshly made eggs and sausage and when the cook went to refuse, he kept his tone quiet which was infinitely more authoritative than if he'd shouted.

Brad Levard, the floor manager, strode in, making a beeline in my direction, his face so thunderous I imagined lightning strikes emanating from his head. "What sort of shit are you pulling?" He'd never liked me since I'd ignored his very obvious attempt to hit on me the day I began work on his floor. Mistakenly, I'd believed his feelings would be less hurt if I'd ignored him instead of giving him the brush off or a polite refusal. My belief was wrong.

I jumped up as he approached my table, earning a stern rebuke from the canteen counter. I was commanded, "Sit!" Mr. P. intercepted Levard before he even reached me, holding out his hand in a warm greeting. Peering at his name tag, he said, "Mr. Levard…Brad. I'm Dr. Crichton. Fortunately, I was in the store shopping when this young man collapsed. I know an organization such as yours would not want any fuss so I brought him in here." Placing his arm across Levard's shoulder in a comradely gesture, Mr. P. steered him away from me as Curried Pearl delivered my breakfast with a flourish. We called her that because she always smelled of whatever was on the lunch menu. Usually curry. She gave me a wink and a nudge, adding "He's a real keeper that one, eh?"

I must have blushed because she went back to the till cackling like a hen about to lay the golden egg.

Mr. P. spoke confidentially to Levard, but loudly enough that I could make out what he was saying. "You know how litigious people are these days and I thought it prudent to short circuit that possibility, that's why I brought him in here out of the public gaze. You don't want Health and Safety throwing their weight around."

"Quite right, Dr. Crichton. The management appreciates your diligence."

"If I may make a suggestion…"

I wanted to make a suggestion myself. Get your arm away from Levard, who seemed to be enjoying the intimacy far too much for my liking, and put it around me.

Please.

"Suggest away," Levard replied with just a hint of flirtation, obviously hoping the suggestion might include the chance of getting to know the doctor a little better.

"The young chap's blood sugar seems to be abnormally low which is why I took the liberty of ordering him a few carbs to get it back up to within normal range…"

"Very good idea," Levard clucked as if he knew fuck all about medicine.

"I think if he may be permitted to stay off the floor for about half an hour to recoup his strength—"

Levard drew breath to reply, but Mr. P. added quickly, "I know, I know what you are about to say. It's a very busy period for you and the young lad is one of your very best workers…"

I almost choked. My superpowers don't include the ability to read thoughts but I can absolutely guarantee that my being a good worker didn't feature anywhere in Levard's mind.

The floor manager was vacillating in his concern.

Mr. P. easily persuaded him back on side. "I'll tell you what. I'll stay here with the lad until he's fit to return to work and then I'll come to your office, with your permission of course, and give you a full debrief. If you like, I could pop in each day and, if you have time from your very busy schedule, we could perhaps have a coffee and discuss his progress."

Oh, Happy Homos, Robin. I'll get to see him every day. I wonder does that include weekends.

He was laying it on a bit thick. I wasn't sure Levard would fall for it, but a manly squeeze of his shoulders and the floor manager capitulated.

"That sounds like an excellent solution to me. I'll be in my office when you're through here."

Said the spider to the fly.

Levard gave me a cheery wave as he left the canteen, while Mr. P. slid into a chair opposite me. I held out my hand. He looked at me, his handsome features screwed up with confusion.

"Well, Dr. Crichton, aren't you going to take my pulse?"

Discover for yourself, it's racing.

He laughed. "I'm not a doctor."

There goes my chance to impress the parents by marrying a medico.

"No shit, Sherlock," I said. It came out a bit snarkier than I intended. "Look, I'd better get back to work; Thel can't handle all those kids on her own."

"You stay right where you are."

He was so authoritative, I got hard.

"If I have to put up with half an hour of that slimy Levard then the least you can do is make it up to me by having breakfast with me first."

"And that would make it all worthwhile?"

"Oh, yes. Very worthwhile."

Shiver me timbers and call me Shirley, I do believe the man is flirting with me.

"What are you doing this weekend?" The smile that accompanied his question made me lose my sense of decorum.

"Why? Are you asking me out on a date?"

"I've never asked a man out on a date before."

Don't say it, Kaz.

But I did. "Why not?"

"You want me to ask you out on a date?"

Is the sky blue? Does bacon on a string pass straight through a goose?

"It would sure do wonders for my image."

"Not sure what it would do for mine."

Ouch.

At least he was still smiling.

"But seriously, what are you doing on the weekend?"

"I was serious," I muttered to myself, but the look of surprise on his face suggested he just might have heard me. If he did, he let it pass.

"I'd like to make you a proposition. I'll make it worth your while."

I was taken aback. "When people proposition me, money is usually not involved, unless it's taxi fare home."

He seemed genuinely perplexed, and then blushed to the roots of his hair. "What? Oh god, no. Sorry, don't misunderstand me. I am an awkward klutz sometimes. Not that sort of proposition. I mean a real job." He looked at the expression on my face. "I've just made it worse, haven't I?"

I nodded my head, my feelings fighting for space among my toes in my elf boots.

He took a deep breath. "Hi, my name is Patric Charles Crichton, no k on the Patric. What can I say? My parents were pretentious. I'm thirty-three years old and I'm offering you employment at a children's Christmas/birthday party this coming weekend because I admire the way you handle the little bastards in large numbers."

Effective way to get me onside then offside in the same breath.

"No thanks," I said, turning my back on his attitude. "I'd better get back to work."

I'd only taken a few steps when he stopped me in my tracks with, "The job pays…" then mentioned a figure so high it took my breath away.

"Exactly who do I have to kill?" I asked.

His laugh echoed around the canteen, causing Curried Pearl to drop a metal tray which clanged to the tiled floor. Laughter was not exactly an everyday occurrence among the nondescript plates and cutlery and the warmed up remnants of what once passed as edible sustenance.

"You obviously don't know your own worth," he said. "That's the going rate for what I'm asking you to do."

I swallowed, both the lump in my throat and my pride. "Upper or lower end of the going rate?"

"It's about the middle."

"What do I have to do?"

"A car will call for you on Saturday morning, bring you to the party where you'll entertain about two dozen kids from mid-afternoon until the early evening, that's when Santa will arrive. You just have to help him cope with the crowds. Then you can join us for dinner and stay the night, take advantage of the facilities, and a car will take you back home the next day. Or, if you wish, the car can take you back after your job is finished on Saturday night."

"And there's no surrendering of body parts to keep alive an ageing patriarch or the slow extraction of all my blood?"

"Now there's a thought," he said.

I didn't want this job under false pretenses. "You must know it would take me six weeks to earn that sort of money here."

"That's because your skills are under-valued."

"Or other people are taking advantage of your gullible nature," I suggested. "I'll tell you what, I'll do it for half what you're offering, and we'll call it a deal. That's how much it's really worth."

"I can afford to pay you," he said, puzzled by my attitude.

"No, we'll do it my way or not at all."

"All right, we'll do it your way."

He got me to jot down my address, suggesting a time that I should be ready, although I immediately wished I had suggested making my own way or having the car pick me up on the corner somewhere far away from my depressed neighborhood.

I felt that even more keenly when the following Saturday a limo arrived. I heard a vehicle pull up in a neighborhood that usually rang to the sound of clapped-out bombs that wheezed down the road at snail's pace held together with hope and the leftovers of last year's pay packet, or else rocked to the beat of loud techno music as they boasted their alpha superiority by performing wheelies, leaving a wake of smoke and particulate rubber on the asphalt. I thought Patric, Mr. P., might call personally but he obviously had a party to organize.

Calling to the driver from my window, I told him to wait, I would be right down. That was no lie as I'd been up and ready since daybreak, nervous as the Bride of Frankenstein before she met her mate. I feared, too, that if the driver strayed too far from his vehicle we might turn up at the party in a limo minus its hub caps. They were an official currency in these parts.

The trip itself was uneventful, taking a little over an hour to the outskirts of the city where a large Victorian mansion awaited my presence. It was just dilapidated enough that I found it fascinating, full of character, and an ideal model for the villa I was having problems with in my Mr. Perfect comic. I was pleased with my prescience in bringing paper and art materials. Perhaps Patric would let me sketch him, provided his wife didn't mind. I was under no illusions in that department. I knew I was here to entertain his son, Damien, and his friends and that there were no sexual overtones connected with my visit.

I could live with that. I'd take the cash and run, after doing my darnedest to make the Christmas party the best I could. Mr. P. came out to meet the car when it pulled up on the gravel driveway outside the main weathered wooden door that had all the cracked and flaky majesty of an ageing diva.

He was all smiles. "Welcome, glad you could make it."

His greeting puzzled me. "You sent a car. Were you expecting it to break down on the way?"

"No, sorry. You'll have to forgive me if I'm a little distracted. Here, let me carry your bags up to your room." He picked up my canvas bags, straining to lift the larger of the two. "What have you got in here? An elephant?"

"I never travel anywhere without all the necessaries. Sorry, it's heavy."

Once he'd shown me into the vast tiled foyer and closed the front door, plunging us into the gloom of dark wood paneling and heavy velvet curtains so redolent of Victorian fussiness I expected to see maids and manservants bustling about to keep the mansion functioning, he put the bag down.

"Listen, there's something I must tell you about this afternoon. But not here. Come with me."

I wanted nothing better than to open the curtains and windows to let in light and air, but I knew my place, so I followed him down the corridor like the governess in Henry James's ghost story, *The Turn of the Screw*. Melodramatic? Certainly, but with an ounce of truth as Mr. P. explained once we were in the book-lined library. I refrained from that old cliché, "Have you read all these?", because the leather bindings revealed they were inherited rather than purchased recently. I was pleased to see a few books on an antique side table alongside a comfortable old grandfather of an armchair situated beneath a reading lamp.

He hesitated between the armchair and the more modern chrome and leather seat behind his desk. Professionalism won over friendliness and he sat behind the large wooden desk, reinforcing the gap between us. I took a seat situated conveniently to give Mr. P. dominance. As it was on wheels, I moved it so that he had to turn to address me. He was irritated at my impertinence but, what the hell, I wasn't here to play games. Well, not with him anyway.

Whether he was wrestling with what he wanted to say or whether he was attempting to control his temper at my temerity I could not tell, but the silence became uncomfortable. I had examined the bookshelves a number of times from my seat and was about to start on the ceiling when he finally spoke.

"I may have lured you here under false pretenses," he said at last.

I certainly hope so. And, yes, I will marry you.

He obviously didn't hear my thoughts because he continued in a totally irrelevant vein.

"To put it frankly, Damien is not exactly the most popular pea in the pod."

He seemed relieved to have unburdened himself of that piece of news. I did wonder, though, how the kid could possibly have inherited a charisma bypass with Mr. P. as his dad.

"The other children tolerate him because their parents tell them to. He's even more morose this year because his mother is away on assignment and won't be coming home for the usual Christmas celebrations although she's managed to organize a hook-up from wherever it is in the world she is."

My look of surprise must have galvanized him into explaining further.

"Sorry. There's no reason you would know his mother is Endive Veroche."

My mouth dropped open in surprise. And admiration. Mr. P. was married to the most important war photographer of the modern age? I was stunned. Everyone knew her work. I understood now, too, why Mr. P. and Damien may not know the exact location of their nearest and dearest. She worked undercover, never embedded with allied troops because, she maintained, they just fed her bullshit. She preferred to branch out on her own recording the day-to-day atrocities of a war zone. She was probably on the hit list of both sides.

"I'm impressed," I managed to say.

"Well, Damien's not. Of course, he's too young to understand and he's becoming more and more withdrawn as the days go by, therefore alienating further those few acquaintances that he does have. So today's party is of the utmost importance if not to him, then to me. It has to turn around the other children's perceptions of him."

"Oh, good, make it easy for me," I said sarcastically. "Don't pile on the pressure."

"I don't expect miracles," he said.

"Not like raising someone from the dead, just a minor loaves-and-fishes style of rabbit-out-of-hat miracle."

"No, the party's catered."

I laughed at his little joke but failed to find anything about this situation amusing.

"I'll show you to your room. It's yours for as long as you stay. It may look as if the house should have a lot of servants but those days are long gone. There's a cook comes in to make breakfast and she's a stickler for punctuality. If you want a hot breakfast, you must be at table before 8am or it's leftovers for you. For today, there will be ample food catered, so just help yourself. By all means, set a plate aside in the refrigerator if you wish. Ah, here's your room."

He showed me into a magnificently furnished boudoir, the bathroom of which would have contained my entire bedsit. "Oh, my," I sighed. "It's magnificent. I feel like Norma Shearer in *Marie Antoinette*. I love it."

He seemed surprised by my enthusiasm.

Hustling me out, he pointed to his room at the end of the hallway, before climbing up a flight of stairs to what looked as if it had once been servants' quarters although now converted into a nursery-cum-play area. "Of course, you have the run of the house and the grounds," he explained, "but as best you can keep the children away from the kitchen. Oh, and the library. If you need anything, that's where you'll find me. Any questions?"

"What time is Santa arriving?"

"About 4 o'clock. See if you can get them to have a nap before he arrives. Their parents will pick them up around six."

I accompanied him downstairs to grab my bag and haul it to my room where I spilled the contents all over the bed in a flurry of activity. I had requested that Mr. P. buy a few items to which he readily agreed and I took them up to the Secret Room as I renamed it and set about my preparations, occasionally popping back to my bedroom when I needed further inspiration.

I was in the middle of transforming the upstairs room when I heard a little voice behind me. "What are you doing?"

I turned to study the forlorn little figure. "I'm getting everything ready for your party."

"They don't like me, you know." Such a sad little boy, and only six years old. Time enough to be disappointed when you reach adulthood. Still, I wouldn't lie to him and hope that would make everything better.

"Then we'll just have to get them to change their minds, won't we?"

"How?"

He was inquisitive, so there was still hope.

"See that packet over there?" He nodded. "Can you write your name?"

"Of course." He was indignant that I would even doubt it for a moment.

"In that case, I want you to pick out one of the T-shirts in the packet, they're all the same, and then I want you to write your name in really big letters on the front and the back. Think you can do that?"

I handed him a black marker pen, watching as he chose his shirt carefully then sat on the floor, his tongue poking out of the corner of his mouth in concentration as he laboriously wrote his name. When he completed the task, he held it up proudly.

"Good boy. Now hand me the shirt and you take a seat just over there and try not to move for a few minutes. Got that?"

"I'm not stupid," he admonished me.

"Sorry," I said.

He took a seat looking very stern. I searched his face for traces of Mr. P., but could see none. He must take after his mother. With a few quick strokes of the pen, I had drawn his likeness, holding it up for his approval.

"Is that me?" he asked.

"Uh huh. Try it on and go and have a look at yourself in the mirror over there."

I helped him pull the T-shirt over his head; it was adult sized so it fitted him like a smock, which was my intention. He stood admiring himself and his drawn likeness for an age, and then he said, "Cool. Can I keep it?"

"It's all yours. But take it off now because you'll need it for the party."

I helped him when he struggled to remove it by himself. He folded it, placing it over a chair.

"Can I help?" he asked, coming back to my side, definitely more involved now.

"Of course, I'd like that."

The preparation time rushed by so that I was still putting the finishing touches to everything when I heard the first cars arrive. The playroom overlooked the front of the house and we could hear none-too-excited voices complaining they didn't want to be here, begging to be taken home. I marveled at Damien's equanimity under such a barrage of negativity and attempted to save what little of his dignity remained by talking loudly enough to drown out their voices.

"It's all right," he said. "I know they didn't want to come to my party."

"Time to put your special shirt on. I'll put mine on as well." Mine had a caricature of me, my features much more exaggerated than Damien's; his was as lifelike a portrait as I could make it.

I took his hand as we went downstairs to greet the guests, feeling the tension in his grip. The parents put on a brave face as they deposited their unwilling offspring. Mr. P. must have heard the hubbub because he made a special guest appearance greeting the mainly mothers by first name, some of them flirting openly with him. A few asked after Endive, they and their children scrupulously avoiding Damien until one little girl pointed at his T-shirt of which he'd become inordinately proud and said sarcastically, "What is that you're wearing?"

The other boys and girls, busy until then playing games or texting on their mobile phones, looked up.

The parents all turned to stare at Damien. Mr. P. looked to me for an answer.

"That's part of this afternoon's activities," I said. "Part of the games."

Some of the parents gave me a sympathetic smirk, while others smoothed out party dresses that cost more than a week's wages for me, or attempted to pat down unruly hair on the boys. The children were all between five and seven but it was the males who looked most unhappy to be there. This group was going to take some winning over, something Mr. P. must have realized as he bid goodbye to the parents and fled back to the safety of the library.

When I was finally alone with the kids, I corralled them upstairs to wait outside the door to the playroom upon which I'd taped a very large sign dominated by a rough illustration of children having old-fashioned fun. No sooner had we reached the door than some of the guests recommenced playing with their mobiles.

"Right," I said to gain everyone's attention. "From this point on, all phones off!"

"What if we don't want to?" one little boy piped up.

"Let me see," I said in my most cordial manner. "You're all grown-ups here, so I'll treat you like grown-ups." A few chests thrust out in pride. "You make your own decision about your phones. If you want to come inside and play, then turn your phone off and then seal it in one of those envelopes after you write your name on it. Otherwise, you can sit out here or down in the foyer and wait for your parents to come and pick you up. Right?"

"What's inside?" one of the girls asked.

"Games," I said.

"Computer games?"

"No, old-fashioned games. Come on, who's coming in?"

Three of the boys shrugged, switched off, then sealed the phones in one of the envelopes each. As instructed, Damien led them into the room, instructing them to write their names on a T-shirt. He closed the door behind him.

"Anyone else?"

One of the girls stepped forward but her best friend stamped her foot impatiently and squealed, "Debbie!"

But Debbie was not for turning and I soon let her into the room to join the very small party indeed. There were twenty in all, including Damien, and so far, only five were inside. I had taken a calculated risk but I knew I had to separate the guests from their electronic distractions. Don't get me wrong, I have no beef with modern technology when it's used for good but when it becomes an anti-social device, then look-out kids!

It took a further twenty minutes after I closed the door on the hold-outs before they all ventured inside lured no doubt by the gales of genuine laughter from those favored few inside. They came in dribs and drabs, the final hold-out, not unexpectedly, being the rude little girl from the initial meeting at the front door. She sulked into the room and rather than make a big fuss I spirited her straight over to the T-shirts and got her to write her name then sketched the most flattering portrait I could. She baulked at wearing it as her mother had obviously gone to a lot of expense to doll her up, but when I insisted she would have to go back outside, she relented begrudgingly. She soon overcame her snit, fortunately, and joined right in.

The T-shirts served a two-fold purpose: to keep the children's good clothes from getting soiled and to give me a reminder of their name.

The games we played were fairly conventional but their newness to these children was such that they enjoyed them out of all proportion to their origins. Once they were exhausted from all their screaming and running about inside, I took them outdoors, still without their phones, in order to explore the lawns and gardens for insects and bugs from which I wove a fantasy story about fairies who lived among the flowers and elf princes who rode snails like wild water buffalo and which I illustrated on my giant draft-paper pad.

It was an absolute joy to see the kids getting their hands dirty. I marched them off to the bathroom to wash up when catering arrived. We set up trestle tables on the lawn and gave the children blankets to lay about on in the shade because the sun was scorching hot that summer. Mr. P. joined us for the food which I'd insisted be healthy with a minimum of sweet, sugary biscuits and lollies. To deflect any young complaints, I'd had each of the children pick a flower or leaf from the garden, telling them that the caterers would cook it up in the big kitchen inside and bring it out for all to share.

Admittedly, there was a degree of skepticism when a rose petal re-emerged as tomato flans, and a cicada shell transformed into vol au vents, dandelions into small quiches, but they ate them anyway. The caterers boxed up each child's garden choice with a couple of examples of what it had transformed into to take home with them along with a piece of the delicious tiramisu birthday cake.

Mr. P. sang louder than all of us when the cake appeared with its six bright sparklers instead of candles, the partygoers oohing their wonder. I told Damien to blow them out when I judged they'd just about sparkled themselves to death, and he made his wish, screwing his eyes up tightly. Then he ran back to join a group who welcomed him with a warmth that had been sadly lacking earlier in the day. Some of the girls sought him out to talk to him which was such a turn around that Mr. P. looked at me as if I had some sort of magical powers.

"I knew I made the right choice," he said before heading back inside the house.

I regretted he didn't have more time for his son but many adults lack the patience for hours of exhausting game playing. After they had finished their snacks and their fruit juices it was time to head back inside for a nap. It would also give me a chance to recharge my batteries which were seriously in danger of running out of energy.

When the youngsters were all asleep, I crept out to make my way downstairs to the library where Mr. P. was engrossed in paperwork when I tapped on the door and entered.

"Ah, Kaz," he said, pausing in the midst of an important pile of documents.

"They're all napping," I said by way of explanation.

"Any problems?" he asked.

"In the beginning. Nothing I couldn't handle though."

"Damien?"

"He seems to be having a ball. He's made a few friends. I think they might stick."

"That is a miracle in itself." He sat back in his chair. "I hope you'll do me the honor of joining me for dinner."

"Yes, I'd like that," I said.

"Good," he replied then went back to his paperwork signaling our little chat was over.

I went back to the play room and was soon as fast asleep as my charges only snapping out of it when I felt a small body jump on my chest. They would definitely be friskier after their sleep and I had to channel that energy or it would be the end of me. Seating them in a semi-circle, I had them call out their favorite animal, real or mythological, and then directed them to the large sheets of paper and paints, the other items I had asked Mr. P. to buy, to draw the animal they'd named, explaining it should be a large picture so they could see it from the air. I thought they may have guessed they were drawing a design on what would become home-made kites, but they painted on blissfully unaware. When they finally twigged, there was a hush of disbelief that they could actually make their own playthings. They had only ever heard of store-bought toys.

With perseverance, and a lot of help from me, each child eventually created something approximating a kite, weird and wonderful though they were. It didn't matter whether they flew or not, it was the excitement of having created something themselves. In the event, they all flew even if only for a matter of seconds but no one minded as they were having too much fun running around the lawns dragging their kites behind them, making enough noise to be heard on the moon.

They were still at it when the limo came back with Santa seated regally in the back. Kites forgotten they ran after him until I managed to calm down their unruly behavior. Santa was a consummate professional, listening to each and every child's request, gently steering them away from impossible gift ideas, like the boy who wanted a real sabre sword to chop up his teachers at school. He gave out a small gift to each of them after they'd solemnly sworn to him that they'd been good all year.

When he'd finished I took him down to the library where Mr. P. had drinks and a little food waiting for him. I went out to the lawn to gather up the kites just as the cars started arriving to pick up the partygoers. I gave each child his or her kite plus their mobile as their parents arrived.

Damien stood proudly in the driveway saying his farewells to everyone while some of the guests bombarded their confused parents with requests that they invite Damien to their Christmas party because they'd had so much fun at his. A few of them looked at me suspiciously as if wondering what strange power I'd used on their child.

Not all of them would reciprocate, just enough that Damien would no longer be a pariah. One little girl even ran over to peck him on the cheek and although Damien made a big deal of wiping the kiss off with his sleeve there was no disguising his secret delight. I scooted him off to his bedroom after everyone had left in order that I could debrief with Mr. P. but when I opened the library door, he was nowhere to be seen. Santa, still in costume, savoring an amber liquid topped with ice, waved me in.

"Sorry," I muttered. "I was looking for—"

"Come in, lad," he said. "Close the door. Mr. Crichton said for you to wait for him in here. Care for a drink?"

"Uh, no thanks."

"I hear very good things about the way you handled the children before I arrived. They were very docile in comparison to some of the other groups I've had."

"Thanks," I said, warming to him.

"So what can old Santa bring you for Christmas? Is there something you want above all else?"

I snickered. If only Santa knew.

"That was a very dirty laugh, lad. Come on, spit it out!"

"As long as Santa won't be shocked," I said.

"Ha. Nothing shocks this old Santa. I've heard just about everything. If it's that shocking come and whisper it in my ear."

I found myself walking over to him. What the hell was I thinking?

"Park your butt here, young man," he said patting his knee.

I did it automatically as if I were a young child again.

"So tell me what it is you most desire in the world."

He looked so comforting I couldn't help myself.

"More than anything in the world, right now I want Mr. P."

"Who's Mr. P.?" he asked.

"Patric."

"Mr. Crichton? Your boss?"

"Mmm."

"Why do you call him Mr. P.?"

I explained about my comic hero, Mr. Perfect, and how much I'd modeled him on Patric. I rambled on and on, hoping I wasn't embarrassing myself, but the old guy chuckled conspiratorially.

"Why don't you tell him?"

"He wouldn't be interested in me. A hot guy like that. I'm just a scrawny stick. He's smart…" I was going to go on and on about Patric's good points but I thought that was probably unwise.

"Is it his money you're after?"

"Has he got money? It can't be much; this old place is falling down round his ears. It's a lovely old house though."

"If it's not his money, you after an overnighter or for keeps?"

"For keeps would be nice."

"What if he doesn't do for keeps?"

"Then I'd settle for once. I can't stop thinking about what it would be like."

"Here, son, close your eyes, make a wish and put your hand in here."

I should have known. This guy was just another filthy old Santa turned on by having a young guy perched on his knee. Before I could stand up, Santa grabbed my hand and pulled it toward him, thrusting between the buttons on his jacket, through the rent in his fat suit. Okay so the guy wasn't as fat as he looked, big deal, he was still a sleaze.

I was surprised when my hand reached bare skin: hard, muscular flesh. I stopped struggling, running my fingers from the guy's muscular chest down over his hardening nipples to his abs. Oh my God! Santa's got a six-pack! But he hadn't finished with me yet, guiding my hand a little lower until it reached a very hard cock poking up toward his navel.

I withdrew my hand as if I'd been burned.

"What's the matter, you don't like?"

Santa was an old fraud. I pulled his beard off to reveal Mr. P.'s laughing face.

"You bastard," I cursed. "That was a mean trick."

"It's only mean if Santa doesn't grant your wish."

I was still on his knee. He had an erection. I had an erection. What more did I need to think about? I grabbed Santa's face and planted the sloppiest, tonguiest kiss on his mouth that I could manage, while I unbuttoned his jacket to get my hands on those fabulous abs again.

It was fun playing with his muscles but I was after that jutting monster between his legs. I pulled down Santa's baggy trousers and palmed his cock which was already straining for release. He attempted to stand up to remove his pants totally but I pushed him back in his seat. I had enough leeway to suck his brains right out of his skull via his prick. That's how determined I was at that moment. I nuzzled his balls with my nose and lips, before working my way slowly up his shaft, thumbing his slit, admiring his large cut cock, happy to spend the night worshipping it.

Eager to taste him, I slid my lips over the crown, suctioning down as far I could without opening my throat just yet. That was a gift for later, once I brought him to a peak. He seemed content to sit back and watch me while I paid homage to his beauty. He wasn't arrogant, just superior as if the world owed him their sexual obedience. Who was I to argue when the object of my lascivious thoughts was within blowing distance?

"It's been so long," he groaned, as he ran his fingers through my hair.

In that case, it was time to reveal my true talent. I took a deep but silent breath before I plunged downward not stopping until his prick was pushing into my throat. Controlling my gag reflex, I bobbed in short arcs to keep him wedged tight until I needed to breathe. He grasped the arms of the chair as if an electric shock had surged through his body.

"That is truly spectacular," he sighed.

If that wasn't a signal to do it again, I don't know what would be. I went back to ministering to his needs, his cock constricting my throat until I thought I would burst. I didn't know how long I could keep this up but I reasoned that as he'd asked me to stay the night that this was but a preliminary round.

Giving it my all, I bobbed until his cock was buried as deep as it could go, using my tongue, my teeth, every oral trick in my armory, until he called out as if in pain and I felt his spunk squirt down my willing throat. I regretted that I didn't get to taste him but his obvious relish of my skills offset that disappointment. Plus the fact I would get to taste him later.

"That was absolutely amazing," he said.

"Would you like a repeat?"

"Later," he puffed. "Let me get my breath."

Then I was hoping he might take care of the throbbing I had between my legs.

"If you were interested, why didn't you say something before?" I asked.

"I didn't want to jeopardize Damien's party," he said. "That was the most important thing. But now that's out of the way—"

"There's nothing stopping us."

"Plus I had to be sure you were really interested—"

"Could I have made it any more obvious?"

"I thought you may have been after me for my money?"

"Why, have you got tons of the stuff?"

He stilled my wandering hands, holding my wrists together, making me look him in the eyes. "You really don't know who I am, do you?"

"Holy Batcrap, you're a serial killer or a vampire or some shit like that, aren't you? And I'm in deep trouble?"

"Nothing like that. I'm Patric Charles Crichton. Head of PCC Industries."

"OMG!" I screamed. "Not the Patric Charles Crichton of PCC Industries?"

I had no idea what the fuck his name meant, so I laid it on thick. His smile of satisfaction showed I'd done the right thing.

"So you can see why I'm a bit wary of getting involved with just anyone."

I let go of his cock which I'd been pumping slowly while we got the talk out of the way. His idea, not mine. The talk part of it. "Why don't you open your mouth a bit wider and insert the other foot?"

That took his breath away. I stood up, gathering my clothes.

"Just for the record, your name and the name of the company mean nothing to me so, big shot, save the self-importance for the people who are impressed by that sort of pompous priggery, like those puffed-up harridans who brought their poor kids here today. I wanted you because I liked you. Get it? I don't suppose you do. Oh, and by the way, yes, I got those none-too-subtle hints you dropped as Santa Claus that just maybe Mr. Perfect was not into relationships. Still I was willing to settle for an overnighter if that's all I could get. Because I like you. Make that liked. You're so far up your own fundament, you can't see what's in front of you. No wonder Damien's so screwed up."

That was below the belt but I was angry as hell.

"And how patronizing can you be?" I was like a dog with a bone and not about to give up. "You don't want to get involved with 'just anyone'? How about I just duck home to get my vaccination certificates, my passport, my driver's license, my employment record, my college exam results, and my criminal record so you can make an informed decision? Then, how about you do the same for me so I know I'm not sucking 'just anyone'!"

He seemed shocked. "You've got a criminal record?"

"See? No, I don't have a criminal record; I was trying to make a point. I thought you were a free spirit but you're even more timid and uptight than all the others." I was dressed by this time. "If you don't mind, I won't be staying the night. I'd like to leave."

I didn't exit grandly like Norma Desmond; I shuffled out in case I burst into tears. How could my Mr. P. go from Perfect to Puerile in such a short period of time? Upstairs, I packed quickly, sitting in my room hoping he had called the limo back because there was no way I was staying under the same roof that night.

About twenty minutes later, there was a knock at the bedroom door. I dreaded facing Mr. P. again but I took a deep breath, wiped my eyes, and answered. It was the limo driver.

"Seems I have another passenger going back? You about ready?"

Of course, Santa was still here. I grabbed my bags, the limo driver helping me with the heavier one, and we manhandled it down the stairs. As we passed the library, I couldn't help but call out loudly enough that he'd hear me. "Do you want to come out and search my bag, just in case I'm stealing any of the cutlery?"

I heard a crash of something breaking from inside the closed room.

"Ouch," the limo driver commented.

Santa was waiting for me in the limo, already helping himself to the alcohol for the long ride back. His name was Colin and by the time we reached the city proper, and my place in particular, we were the best of drunken mates, so much so the limo driver had to help me up to my bedsit, leaving Santa as hubcap guard. Patting my ass, the driver lay me down on the bed fully dressed.

"Don't think I'm not tempted, mate, but I don't take advantage of the inebriated. Maybe if we run into each other under different circumstances…"

He let himself out leaving me to sweet oblivion until I woke up the next day with a Holy Batcrap of a head.

I was sick, so sick, physically and psychically. The physical demanded immediate attention, my head poised over the toilet bowl and then a long draft of seltzer to settle my stomach and a handful of aspirin for my head, the psyche having to be stored away for later. The remainder of the day was spent feeling sorry for me and wondering if I was going to die.

Here lies the body of our dear departed son, Kaz, who remained undiscovered because no one even missed him.

I couldn't believe my head was still pounding. I just wanted it to stop. Not only was my head jabbering like a jackhammer, I was now hearing voices. "Kaz, open up. If you don't open up soon I'll break the bloody door down. Come on, it's Thel."

What? The voice inside my head was a trannie named Thel?

I sat bolt upright in bed, regretting it immediately. I groaned, stumbled out of bed, and unlatched the door, letting Thel push her own way in while I collapsed again.

"What are you doing here?" I groaned.

"When you didn't turn up for work, and didn't ring in, I was worried."

"What do you mean work, it's Sunday?"

"It's late Monday afternoon and Levard is spitting chips. You'll be lucky to have a job come tomorrow." Thel went to the bathroom and turned on the shower. "Right, now you can get yourself into the bathroom and scrub up or you can give Thel a cheap thrill and make me undress you and shove you in the shower. Your choice."

I was unsteady on my feet, but determined. "Loath as I am to deprive you of an opportunity to feast your eyes on my privates…"

"Good boy. You must be getting better if you can string a sentence together that long without stuttering. Now scoot."

The shower was the first step in my recovery, the second was going out for a cheap meal with Thel. I explained what had happened over the last few days, not sparing my own stupidity from her derision, but instead I got sympathy.

"He seemed like such a nice man, too. Not at all like I expected."

"What do you mean?"

"You really don't know who he is? That wasn't all an act?"

"Have you ever known me to act that well?"

"No, love, your feelings are always plastered all over your face."

"So, who is he?"

"Worth a fortune if the papers are to be believed. Gives a lot of it away to good causes."

"So he's a philanthropist?"

"Wouldn't know about his religion, they never mention that. He's a bit of a recluse."

"No wonder he doesn't date."

"Must be scary to have that much money," Thel sighed, probably wishing just for once in her life she could be that frightened.

The remainder of the meal was taken up with small talk while at the back of my brain, my conscience was attempting to work out whether I had wronged the man. It was a moot point as I'd never see him again to apologize whatever the outcome of the moral dilemma.

When it came time for Thel to return to her long-suffering boyfriend I went to pay the bill over her objections only to discover an envelope in my coat pocket, an envelope stuffed with cash. I saw her to the train then raced back to my bedsit not daring to count the money in public.

The limo driver must have put the envelope in my coat when he walked me up to my apartment. I couldn't believe my sudden wealth. It was the full amount that Mr. P. had suggested, not my lower acceptance. I wrestled with my conscience for a few seconds until I overpowered it for the mandatory count of ten then put the money aside for a rainy day. Beneath that hot, muscular, cheating exterior, there was a heartless of gold. Besides, I had no way of returning the extra cash.

I looked vainly for a note, so I slept only fitfully that night, my dreams full of my tarnished hero and the wrong I had done him.

Levard was surprisingly sanguine about my no-show the previous day, dismissing my apology airily with the rejoinder, "It's of no importance, Kaz. Dr. Crichton rang in on your behalf saying that he had seen you on the weekend and in his opinion, you were unfit for work yesterday."

My look of surprise didn't seem to register with the floor manager, but at least my job was safe. Thinking it over, that bastard limo driver must have reported back to Mr. P. on my condition. Well, he could make of it whatever he wanted.

Thel welcomed me back like I'd been gone for months instead of just a day and by morning tea she'd cajoled me into my normal childish, good-natured, optimistic self. Optimistic in most respects but not about Mr. P. I didn't want to invest energy and emotions in a relationship with a married man, even if his wife was away most of the year. I wanted a superhero all my own. Was that selfish?

"No, love," Thel said. "That's what we all want, but there should be a rule we can trade 'em in every ten years or so for a better model."

"Ain't that the truth," Curried Pearl added. She had joined our table for her allotted ten-minute break, slurping her coffee like she was drinking it through a straw and smoking like the proverbial chimney even though there were No Smoking signs dotted on all the available wall space between notices for the staff badminton championships and the social club outing to see Mamma Mia.

So the days passed as I marshaled faceless children toward Santa for their three-minutes of annual greed (photograph $10 extra) until a week later a tiny hand tugged at my sleeve. "Damien?" I squatted so I was on the same level.

He was pouting. "You didn't stay for dinner."

"Oh, I'm sorry about that. I had urgent business in town. You were taking a nap when I left and I didn't want to wake you."

It was the truth. I didn't want him to think I'd just walked out on him. I'd done a quick sketch of him sleeping, leaving it on his bedside table so he knew that I cared just a little.

"I know. Patric framed your picture and it's hanging in my room. It's cool."

I didn't want to ask, I really didn't.

"Where is Patric?"

He pointed. There was no use in not turning as the object of our conversation would have noticed we were talking about him. Fortunately for me, Levard was oozing all over him, keeping him distracted.

"Don't you like Patric?" Damien asked.

I was taken aback by the forthright question. Well, yes, I did, do like Patric, k or no k.

Before I had a chance to answer, Damien added. "He misses you."

"And I miss him, too. But don't tell him."

He crossed his heart, although I noticed he had his fingers crossed.

"Did you want to see Santa again today? Did you forget to ask for something?"

"Yes," he said earnestly.

I placed him in the line before returning to my regular duties, making sure to keep an eye open for his welfare as he moved patiently forward. When at last he hopped on Santa's knee, whispering in his ear, I saw him point in my direction. I hoped he wasn't vindictive enough that he was asking Santa for a hit man to take me out.

When he'd finished, I fetched him, offering my hand which he took as I made my way over to Mr. P., my heart beating until I thought I would be unable to go through with the meeting. Both he and Levard turned their beaming smiles in our direction as we approached. Damien pulled at my hand for the last few meters as my feet seemed remarkably reluctant to take the necessary steps.

Mr. P.'s face was a study in neutrality as I nodded my greeting. "Thank you for ringing Mr. Levard to let him know I was feeling unwell last week."

I saw a slight curling of the corner of his mouth on my use of the word 'unwell.'

"That's what…doctors are for," he replied. My heart stopped when he paused, hoping he might say 'friend' but I guess he couldn't. That would be unprofessional. Anyway, I didn't need a common or garden variety friend, I needed a boyfriend. Preferably one who was available.

We stood around awkwardly until I let Damien's hand go to return to my job. I saw the look of distress on Damien's face.

"Ask him Patric, go on." A little voice pleaded.

Mr. P. looked mortified, speaking harshly to his son. "Not now, Damien."

That was my cue to leave and after wishing Damien an effusive goodbye which just seemed to embarrass Mr. P. further, I made a hasty exit. I had no idea what was going on there but I knew it was not a good place to be. Maybe Mr. P. had transferred his affections to the odious Levard. The guy wasn't bad looking but his personality, let's just say, if it came down to a choice between Levard and a cobra, the snake would win every time.

As I went about my shepherding task, I watched as P. shook hands with Levard, leaving the floor without so much as a backward glance although Damien gave a little wave. I waved back. It wasn't his fault his dad was such a bastard. A sweetheart of a bastard.

The afternoon was so busy I had no time to think any further on the matter until my tea break when Thel and I slumped exhausted in the canteen chairs, so over the Christmas bustle we failed to notice how putrid the coffee was.

"There you are, Kaz," one of the friendlier Santas said, plonking himself alongside. "None of my business, but I just thought you'd like to know, that little boy you were so friendly with—"

"Damien. He's a friend's son," I said to clarify my relationship.

"Well, it's just he had a mighty funny Christmas wish. You get all sorts, of course, some would just tear your heart out, but he was very specific. He even offered to give up his other Christmas presents. Most unusual for a little boy to give up presents. But, what I'm trying to say is, when I asked what he wanted for Christmas, he pointed at you and said 'I want him as my daddy.' There you go, for what it's worth."

Oh shit, I had a sudden need to run to the men's room so I could bawl my eyes out in private.

My eyes were still red when I got home in the early evening. I wasn't depressed exactly, just a little heartbroken for Damien, and feeling sorry for myself. I tried working at my drawings, wallowing sufficiently that I didn't hear the tap on the door until it became more insistent. I really was not in the mood for one of the other occupants of the building coming to me to borrow money or ask if I was selling drugs. I ignored it for as long as I could then reluctantly put down my pencil because I was in danger of scribbling all over my portrait of Mr. P. in annoyance and flung open the door.

My first reaction was astonishment, which gave way to embarrassment, in turn becoming irritation, then finally lust. Mr. P. stood at the door to my scummy bedsit. Although all those emotions ran through me in record time, I was still gaping.

"Are you going to invite me in?"

I so much didn't want him to see how I lived, but to have him in the same room as me over-rode my good sense. As I stood aside I was curious. "What are you doing here?"

"To see you, of course. Do you need to ask?"

"Yes, I do. I thought we'd already established I'm not suitable. Oh wait, you would have needed time to check me out first to see that I wasn't 'just anybody'." *I really must to learn to keep my mouth shut.*

I wouldn't have blamed him had he walked out after that welcome but he said simply, "I deserve that. Now it's out of your system, let's move on." Taking in my room, he retaliated with, "I see accommodation for students hasn't improved much since my day." Somehow, though, I just couldn't picture Mr. P. living in such squalor.

"What do you want?"

"I came to invite you out to dinner. At a restaurant."

"You think I need fattening up? Don't let these surroundings fool you."

"No, dammit! A date."

Holy penguins in a burnt butter sauce! Me. On a date. Call the Daily Planet. Hold the presses! Scoop of a lifetime. Kaz asked out on an actual date by the hottest man in the universe…

Unfortunately, Mr. P. chose that exact moment to find the comic book Mr. Perfect, the Hottest Man in the Universe ® ™ (patent pending) who bore a remarkable likeness to his inquisitive self.

"Is this me?"

I didn't dare speak, so I nodded my head.

"What am I supposed to be?"

Clearing my throat, to give myself time to censor my thoughts and give him the family rated version about him and my libidinous superhero, all my reservations went out the door and I babbled away like some stupid kid seeking approval from grownups. In his favor, Mr. P. listened patiently, didn't interrupt the more ludicrous aspects of what I was telling him, until he couldn't stand it any more and he placed his index finger on my lips.

All he had to say was, "I missed you," and I was in his arms.

I was hoping the way I ravaged his tongue was answer enough. I still couldn't believe that he was in my bedsit, that he missed me, and that I was succumbing to a married man.

Ain't love grand?

He backed me onto the bed and began divesting me of my clothes while he shucked off his own shirt and I struggled to undo his belt. "I want you," he muttered, blotting out the few remaining reservations I had. No one had ever wanted me like this before.

He lay on top of me, both of us totally naked after the undignified wriggling to divest ourselves of our clothing, pinning my arms above my head.

He gently bathed my lips with his tongue before gently pushing his way inside, my tongue eager to greet him. There was none of the hurried exploration like the last time we'd found ourselves in this situation.

"Mmm, sweet," he murmured when he came up for air, "I should kiss you more often."

"Make a booking. My dance card is pretty empty at present."

I snacked on his tongue, sliding my lips around it as if it were a cock, rocking back and forth in a facsimile of a blow job. I've had kisses rough and kisses gentle and his was by far the most arousing I'd ever experienced. He took it to a whole new level. I couldn't get enough as he ground his hips against my body in rhythm with his tongue in my mouth. It wasn't all selfish domination because he withdrew to allow me access to his warm wet mouth when I tried so hard to imitate his technique. He was obviously more experienced than me, so I added a small playful flourish. I tickled his gums with my tongue, making him squirm.

He pulled away, disappointing me because I was in no great hurry now that I had him in my bed, but he made me gasp when he ran his lips down my throat and across to my nipple, nibbling at it until it was hard as the tip on a frozen ice cream. He repeated the exercise on the neglected one before burrowing his nose between my feeble pecs then, snorting his breath on my skin, he licked his way down to my navel where he stopped for a brief inspection before continuing farther south, past the pubic jungle, to the leaning tower that was my busting-for-action cock.

Expecting a few tugs with his hand, I was totally unprepared when he opened his mouth and swallowed my prick whole. I called out in surprise, my body bucking on the bed, as his tongue made merry with the underside of my shaft and he bobbed his head up and down to take me to the root. I watched as my dick disappeared between his lips which only made my orgasm even more perilously close. I tried to pull his head away without success so I warned him, "If you keep doing that, I'm gonna come."

He took his mouth off, which gave me a chance to recover, and said, "Can you come more than once a night?"

Does Superman need a new costume designer? Does the Green Lantern need a new color chart? For Mr. P. I could come as many times as he wants.

That ran through my mind. What I said was, "Uh huh."

"Good," Mr. P. replied and went back to his expert blow job, bringing me off in record time and…

Jiminy Grasshopper, he swallows!

I moved on the bed in an attempt to grab his cock, memories of it plowing my throat surfacing in my mind. I was keen to repeat the experience. Unless—

"Lie still," he commanded. "This is all about you tonight."

Even my mind went blank at the thought of that.

"What would you like me to do next?" he asked softly.

You mean apart from move into my bedsit and spend the rest of your life loving me, being my superhero?

"I want you to fuck me," I whimpered.

"You got…?"

I'd already leaned my arm over to the bedside table and fished the makings out of the drawer. He ripped the condom wrapper with his teeth, and then rolled it down his shaft as he asked, "How do you want it?"

This was no time for the obvious smartass answer.

"I want to watch you as you fuck me."

He smiled. "Just the way I like it."

Hoisting my legs onto his shoulders, he slicked my ass with lube, pushing his finger inside so gently I barely felt it. Then a second and a third until I was ready for him.

I was so ready, in fact, that when he aimed his cock at my entrance and pushed, there was hardly any sting at all, and I welcomed his intrusion. As he sank slowly inside me, filling me, I had never felt so at peace. He watched me intently for any signs of discomfort and when he found none he began to thrust, withdrawing until the head of his cock was just inside my sphincter, then sliding back down until he was buried up to his balls.

He was fucking me like a well-oiled machine, deliberately hitting my sensitive spot every third or fourth thrust so I didn't climax too quickly for my cock was hard again. I sighed contentedly because this was so unlike most of the men I picked up who treated screwing as an event on the Spring racing calendar. I squeezed my ass muscles in appreciation and he gasped.

"Do that again and I won't be able to hold off. I want this to last."

I did it a few more times in rapid succession, holding off my natural inclination to pleasure him more. After all, I wanted him inside me forever, maybe with time off for public holidays.

Suddenly, I realized not only was sex the greatest thing ever invented, but it was actually fun. I wasn't gritting my teeth, I wasn't wondering when he would blow and go, I wasn't looking at the clock, and I wasn't even working out in my head what I was going to eat for dinner tonight. I was giving Mr. P. my full attention.

He kissed me as he pumped my ass, the speed increasing, his breath coming in short, sharp bursts. I clung to his body, trying to thrust my ass back to meet his penetration, wanting him farther inside me than was humanly possible. Whimpering, I clung to him never wanting to let go as he bellowed, shuddered, and thrust his load inside me, quivering with each spurt.

I squeezed my ass as hard as I could to milk every drop out of him, until he collapsed on top of me. I caressed his hair and down his back, tracing my fingers lightly over his ass cheeks. It must have tickled because he swatted my hand away.

"I'm crushing you," he said, moving off me and onto his side. He removed the rubber, tossing it in the bin beside the bed. I missed the feel of his strength, expecting him to beat a hasty retreat now that he'd had his fun, but he scooted me over so we could spoon, my ass cheeks rubbing against his slick cock.

"I…"

"Don't talk," he said. "Let's just lie here for a spell. Then you can say whatever is on your mind. Okay?"

"Mmm," I agreed.

We fell asleep in that position, waking up cramped and uncomfortable about an hour later. Still, for all my discomfort, I didn't want to move.

"Shit, I was going to take you to dinner," he said glancing at the clock. "There's still time."

I decided to be selfish. "I'd rather stay in bed with you."

Even though his tummy rumbled, he said, "That would be my choice, too."

My cock strained at the thought of another session with Mr. P. He must have read my mind because, this time, he leaned over to grab another condom from the little pile I'd left on the bedside table.

"Expecting a crowd, were you?" he asked, but he was smiling.

He ripped open the packet, I wriggled in anticipation of another good screwing, but instead of sheathing his dick, he rolled the condom down over my cock.

"What?"

"Keep still, it's your turn."

"But…"

"Don't you want a turn?"

"No one's ever asked before," I said sheepishly.

"I'm asking," he said.

"Yes please," I said, sounding a little bit too much like a kid who's just been asked if he wants an ice cream.

"Let me do it my way first, until I get used to it. Then you can do me any way you like."

I nodded, afraid if I spoke this would all prove to be a dream.

He greased his ass before squatting over my cock, guiding it toward his hole. I lay still, allowing him to do all the work, feeling the tingle as he rubbed it around the entrance to his guts. Working it in slowly, he flinched when it breached the muscle. The last thing I wanted was to hurt him, not that I'm suggesting I'm horse hung or anything, but I couldn't bear to see my Mr. P. in any sort of pain.

Eventually, like all tough guys, he gritted his teeth and got on with it. He plunged down until I was as far inside his ass as I could go. My eyes opened in wonder. So this was why guys were lining up to fuck other guys' asses. Oh, I could totally get used to this feeling.

"Nice, eh?" he grinned. "And I'm not even very good at it. Imagine what an expert, someone like you, could do."

I couldn't have been happier. "You're good enough for me."

"Start slowly," he pleaded.

I moved my hips, pushing in and out of his ass slowly, letting him get used to the feeling. Been there, done that, so I knew what he needed. I tried to keep my rhythm as fluid as possible because the worst kind of screw is from someone who pokes like his cock is stoking a fire in a grate.

Concentrating on finding his little knob of a prostate, I changed the angle of entry ever so slightly until he rewarded me with an expletive so loud they must have heard him downstairs.

"I want you on your back, the same way you did me."

With a minimum of disruption, he leaned back in the bed and held his legs apart. If you've never seen a wall of muscle with his cheeks spread open to take your prick, then you are missing one of the wonders of the world. Mr. P. was offering himself to me and I was gonna take him up on his offer. I was a little less considerate this time, allowing for the fact he'd had time to get accustomed to my dick in his butt. From now on, any man who wanted my ass would have to surrender his in turn.

He grimaced a few times until I heard him expel a deep breath, signaling he had relaxed and was now enjoying the right royal buggering I was giving him.

Does anyone last long their first time? I doubt it, and I wasn't going to be the exception to the rule. Mr. P. stared into my eyes as I rode his ass, more side-saddle than full on home on the range, but I was enjoying myself and I think he was too if the way he was bucking under my inexpert fucking was any indication.

I blurted out, "Sorry," as I increased my thrust, a matter of seconds later spewing my sperm inside him, muttering 'Oh, my god,' over and over until I couldn't squirt any more.

I pulled out slowly, proud of my first effort, grinning sheepishly as I disposed of the rubber. Mr. P. lowered his legs, pulled me to him, sheltering me in his powerful arms. Neither of us needed to say anything and I fell into a contended sleep listening to his heart race in his chest.

I would have been more content if I hadn't awoken the next morning, the right side up in my bed, the sheet and blanket covering my naked body, my hero disappeared.

Too late, I remembered that he didn't do relationships.

It was exquisite agony to get myself ready for work: agony that my body felt like it had been slept in, and exquisite because for a few hours Mr. P. had been mine. He'd shown me more respect than all my other lovers put together, but it galled me that he ran out rather than tell the truth: that our liaison was a one-night fling while his wife was away.

All that was before I discovered he'd stolen the portrait I'd done of him as my superhero. I'd put everything into that. Sure, I could do it again, but I wasn't sure I wanted to any more; it would just serve to open up the wound. I'd try my hand at something else, something more down to earth, more practical.

Fortunately, by the time I got to Santa's Cave my sprits had lifted and the idea of capitulating to the mundane had so horrified me on the bus that I swore to myself I would never travel down that route no matter how appealing it seemed.

I plugged into my memories of Mr. P. whenever I needed a boost to my flagging energy in the lead-up to

Christmas during which the kids seemed to become more unruly and the parents more snarling and unreasonable. Stress compounded, screaming headaches were common place, tempers flared, and I worked with the persistent nagging emptiness where my emotions should be.

Fuck it, I missed him.

Then, all too soon, Christmas Eve rolled around and the thought of the holiday period alone in my bedsit suddenly made me look like a major loser, even to myself. Thel invited me over to her place but she had a large family among whom I'd feel totally out of place. No, I'd sleep in and go to the movies at midday to watch the latest blockbuster, maybe treat myself later to a slap-up burger and fries on the way home.

After we finally saw the last children off for the year, we could have our own little celebration, just a few drinks and canapés before heading home to family. I wouldn't make the mistake this time of imbibing too much although sleeping through the entire day was not without its good points. Even Levard joined our little group complimenting us on what was likely to be the store's best Christmas ever.

"Sorry if I was a little hard on you this year," Levard slurred as he maneuvered me into a corner, placing his arm against the wall so I couldn't escape.

Don't let him proposition me. I want to work here again next year.

I tried to attract someone's attention so they could come to my aid as Levard rabbited on and on about how impressed he was with my commitment which became what a good worker I was and then not-so-subtly morphed into what an attractive young man I was.

Help me!

I noticed everyone had their eyes toward the lift which was behind me, the only sound Levard's inept attempt at a pick-up, until eventually he stopped speaking, his mouth dropping open in surprise. It was Thel's squeal of delight that made me turn.

I'm afraid I gaped, too. Striding toward us was Mr. Perfect. Not Mr. P. but rather my superhero in full costume as I'd drawn it on the sheet that had disappeared along with Patric Charles Crichton from my apartment and my life. My mind noted a few minor adjustments I'd need to make to the costume color scheme and an important one to the cut of the fabric covering his crotch as currently it was much too revealing, especially as Mr. Perfect seemed to be sporting a mammoth erection. I knew from experience it wasn't padding.

I could see determination in his eyes as he pulled me to his body and planted the most sizzling kiss to my lips, raising me off the ground in the process, with scant regard for anyone who was watching. I thought I heard Thel clap but it could just have been the bells that were pealing in my head.

"Damien wants me to bring you home for Christmas," he said simply.

I couldn't help it. "I don't look good in stockings," I replied.

"But you'll look mighty tasty in my bed."

"Once is all right, but twice makes it look like some sort of relationship is developing."

"I missed you."

"Me, too."

He scooped me up in his arms just like a superhero. He spoiled the effect somewhat by walking to the lift rather than flying from the window. I could live with that. I could live with whatever he decided. I would even be the other woman for him.

"What other woman? What are you talking about, Kaz?" He looked genuinely puzzled as the lift ascended to street level.

"Your wife. Damien's mother."

He guffawed fit to piss himself.

"I'm not married, you dickhead. Endive is my sister. Damien is my nephew. I look after him whenever sis is away on assignment."

I tweaked his nipple really hard until it hurt.

"Ow. What was that for?"

"For leading me on. Making me worry."

Deep down I knew he could lead anywhere and I'd follow.

Once we reached the street, passers-by gawped at the strange sight, until a limo pulled up and Mr. P. deposited me in the back seat before wrapping me in his massive arms, planting another of those lip searing kisses on my mouth. As the car pulled out into the late Christmas Eve party-going traffic, I spied a small box stuffed in the belt of Mr. P.'s costume. I could just make out the words 'Extra Sensitive,' and the number 36.

Holy Batcrap, Robin. A happy ending.

CHRISTMAS CAROL

Jazmin Starr

Be careful what you wish for.

Scrooge was right about Christmas. Carol would have muttered 'Bah! Humbug!' if she'd been of a Victorian mind. She didn't need any convincing that sitting at home alone, using her ivory-hued vibrator while watching her rented male-on-male-action DVDs, was preferable to the alternative: Christmas Day with the family. Now she only had to endure her mother's whining recriminations by phone rather than in person. A successful and self-sufficient woman, unlike her obnoxious and dysfunctional siblings, she had the luxury of living an entire continent away, out of reach of family meddling.

Carol had persuaded the family that she was such a pivotal part of the corporate structure, so necessary to the day-to-day running of the giant financial conglomerate for which she worked, she had to be on stand-by over the holiday period in case of a catastrophic meltdown. She may have exaggerated a little. In reality, she was the PA to the head of the Personnel Department. Hardly likely the company was going to recruit this time of the year, but it had suited her purpose to inflate her importance not least so she could remain in her apartment for the entire duration of the season of good cheer.

Her life was just as she wanted it. Well, maybe not quite. She would not have minded if the guy with all the muscles and tattoos who lived in the apartment block across the courtyard from hers had more transparent window shades. She did like to watch a man with muscle in all the right places working out, especially when he was working that big muscle between his legs as he was now. Moisture flooded her thong as she watched the silhouette of him pumping his shaft on the blinds. She got a real kick out of being a voyeur almost as much as she did when she had a long hard cock driving into her cunt like a jack hammer.

She also wouldn't have minded if there had been just a few less gay men living in the area. Not that she was homophobic, she appreciated the eye candy even if it was a flavor she was never likely to sample, but a couple of straight men thrown into the mix just to even up the odds wouldn't hurt now, would it?

Carol was popular with the gay boys of the inner city. Most were on at least nodding terms with her while many were friends who dropped by for gossip and cocktails, or else a shoulder to cry on or an ear to boast to. Their stories sometimes inflamed her to the extent she had to excuse herself to go to the bathroom and have it out with her own aching pussy, plunging her fingers, or her faithful dildo, between her soft folds imagining it was Tom or Boze or Finn doing the honors instead of sitting in her living room going on about their new conquest.

Still, she wouldn't swap her life for anything. She was an independent woman, no matter how much that stuck in her mum's craw, or probably a dried up old spinster to her married-with-five-children evangelical sister who would ring Christmas afternoon, sauced to the gills with the supposedly non-alcoholic punch that her dad surreptitiously lubricated with enough alcohol to kill an elephant. Winnie would do as she always did, crow at her 'barren' sister, going on at such length about the joys of family and motherhood that Carol had concluded long ago she was a very lonely woman behind the façade.

No, for all its faults, Carol was living the life she wanted, even if it meant keeping the family at arm's length. At thirty-six, there was no denying she still scrubbed up pretty presentable. Certainly the men at her work must see something that appealed since they kept hitting on her, making no secret of their desire to get her into bed. Few of them, however, offered more than a hurried meal in a mid-range restaurant that catered for such clientele and then back to her apartment for a quick screw before they went home to the wife and kids.

Sure, she'd succumbed on the odd occasion; when she needed the warmth of another human body rather than the heat of her vibrator. She wasn't averse to using men at their own game. She supposed, in most eyes, that made her shallow but her mind gave a little shrug and the guilt was gone.

Besides, she didn't have time to think about these things now; she had been so preoccupied with her job and hiring the requisite number of porn videos to last over the holiday, especially those with muscle hunks, that she'd forgotten the most important thing, the turkey, her one concession to Christmas. She liked to cook it just the way her mum did, then pig out on Christmas Day but still have enough left over to last until the New Year by which time she'd be so fed up with turkey she wouldn't want to look at another one until the following Christmas. It worked out well.

Hurrying to her favorite store where she knew the produce was fresh, not thawed, she hoped they would have one left. They were pricey but worth the money. As she approached Chuck, the assistant, she spied one still in the refrigerated counter. Chuck was always pleased to see her and they exchanged a few pleasantries before he asked what he could do for her. The only other customer was a rather handsome guy talking to Sal, the second assistant.

"I'd like that one, please," they chorused in unison, indicating the plump turkey sitting in the case. It would have required the precision of an Olympic time piece to work out who had asked first. The guy, who clearly thought he had precedence, was having none of Carol's attitude of 'me first,' while the two shop assistants looked at one another as if wondering whether to call the cops. No doubt they'd seen many a violent fracas break out for much less than the last turkey during the holiday season.

Travis was all polite insistence as the two counter hands waited to see how this dilemma would resolve itself. "I do believe I was here first," he said, his voice steely with the superiority of his cause.

"But I shop here all the time," she said, with equal determination.

Travis turned to the men behind counter. They flinched at being drawn into the argument even though ultimately they would have to make the decision. "Do you have another one out the back?" he asked hopefully. "Or somewhere."

Both men shook their heads, not daring to speak. They didn't want to antagonize Carol, a long-standing customer even though they believed Travis had the moral claim to the turkey.

"Damn," Travis said.

Carol did appreciate the fact he was not throwing his weight around or assuming the moral high ground.

He was attempting to find a mutually satisfactory solution.

Must be gay. She sighed at the loss of another sexy hunk to Gaydom.

"Say, how about we have it cut in half? Would that work for you?" he asked Carol. "I'd have to pad it out with more…" he was already calculating how best to make half a turkey stretch to feed the four who would be at table the next day.

"Look, it's Christmas," Carol sighed. "I don't need a turkey. I'll be home alone anyway. You take it. Wrap up a half dozen of those chicken breasts, Chuck. They'll do me."

"No, I insist you take half," Travis said, turning to address her. He'd been a little frightened of a scene earlier so had focused on the turkey rather than the woman beside him. He didn't want to be intimidated if she was a ferocious negotiator. He was pleased that she seemed very calm and reasonable. He'd already had numerous run-ins during his shopping expeditions that day; another would have sent his head spinning into migraine territory.

Shit! He knew her… "Carol," he said tentatively.

She looked at him, studying his face carefully. Her first reaction was the natural one; he was gorgeous, but unavailable. Though there was something familiar about him. Her brow clouded.

"It is Carol, isn't it?"

"Yes," she admitted reluctantly in case he was a stalker or she had a doppelganger with the same name wandering the city streets.

"You probably won't remember me. My husband and I met you at Roger's party about three weeks ago. We were introduced briefly."

Now she remembered, and she opened her mouth too readily to close it. "Of course, you were with that hunk of beef…" Her hand went to her mouth to stop any more words from tumbling out and embarrassing her even further.

Travis laughed. "Right. Everyone remembers Nico."

She more than remembered. For the next few days, she made passionate love to the man in her fantasies. He filled her like no other lover before. In fantasy.

"He's your…"

He nodded. "Right. My husband."

Carol was about to mumble some sort of apology although she had no idea what she was sorry for.

"I'm Travis," he said, saving her further embarrassment.

Of course, she remembered him now. He'd allowed Roger to parade Nico around the party as if he were his own personal property. She'd watched Travis, marveling that the guy would allow such a stud out of his sight. If Nico was hers, she'd never let him go.

Chuck cleared his throat.

"Sorry, Chuck. Wrap the damn thing up and give it to Travis. I'll take the chicken."

Travis was about to object but she gave him a severe look which made him change tack. "Look, have you got time for a coffee? It's been fortuitous running into you like this. I have an offer that might solve both our problems."

Carol was perplexed. She didn't know she had a problem.

Asking Chuck to hold both orders until they got back, but paying to make sure a later customer did not purloin them; they adjourned to a café a little farther down the main street. They sat in the cozy interior. Carol ordered a skim milk latte and Travis a hot chocolate. She hated him for not counting the calories and the saturated fats.

"It really was lucky running into you like this," Travis began.

Please don't say it. Please don't say it. Please don't say it, her mind chanted.

"Why don't you come over to our place for Christmas?

Damn! He said it.

She went on automatic pilot to begin listing the myriad reasons on why that would not be possible, but Travis got in first. "Hear me out. This is so not a sympathy invitation."

"Okay, mouth shut until I hear the first sign of something I don't like," she said.

"I know you don't like Christmas, you made that obvious at Roger's party, but we're in an awful jam. Nico's parents are coming to visit him on Christmas Day; their first ever look at his new apartment and, well…"

"Let me guess, they don't know that their son is gay as Lady Ga Ga's groove."

"That about sums it up," he admitted.

"And you want me to do a La Cage aux Folles and pretend to be his girlfriend?"

"Right."

"That is so seventies," she said. "So not cool. Where's your self-respect?"

"I know. I keep telling him to come out to his parents but he's Italian, thinks it will kill them. I even threatened to leave him if he didn't. I got as far as the front door and he was begging me to stay, that he'd tell them. I didn't bother to mention that I was only taking the garbage out. However, I wondered what he would do if I really packed my bags."

"But he never got around to it," Carol surmised.

"Always the excuses."

"So why pick on me?"

"Because you're gorgeous," he said enthusiastically.

Travis certainly had a way with words.

"Um, thanks." She would have preferred to hear it from a straight guy who was flirting with her, not some admittedly hot gay man looking to fool his boyfriend's parents.

"Plus, we sort of know you; you're not a complete stranger. And…"

Carol finished the sentence for him. "Everyone you know is busy on Christmas except me."

"Yeah, that about sums it up."

"As appealing as that offer is–"

And it was tempting. To be the girlfriend of the hottest man in the city. Okay, there was a little hyperbole in there; she hadn't met every man yet, but Nico was certainly up there with the best. Top ten at least. Shame he'd only be her boyfriend for the day and it would only be make-believe anyway. She hummed a few bars of the fifties number It's Only Make Believe, much preferring the original Conway Twitty version to the many later recordings. Although she might have the opportunity to get up close and personal in a platonic way which would feed her fantasies for a few more weeks, she was frightened she might take it too seriously and jump his body.

"Yeah, it sucks. I know."

For a moment, she thought he could read her thoughts.

She said simply, "I have plans."

"Fair enough," Travis sighed, but he passed over his business card after scribbling his home number on the back. "Just in case you change your mind."

She felt obliged to reciprocate, flirting briefly with the idea of making her number illegible or else reversing two of the digits which she could later claim was an accident. That would be childish. He wasn't likely to ring but she may get an invite to a party or two out of it. It paid to have contacts in this city.

"I won't," she said.

"I'd better get back, Nico will be wondering where I am. It was great meeting you again. We should keep in touch."

She liked the non-committal way he said 'should' meaning that if their astrological signs aligned at some distant time they might meet at a party and remember one another.

"Don't forget your turkey," she reminded him as he turned to walk away.

"Shit, thanks," he grinned. "I do feel really bad about taking the last one."

"Just remember, you owe me."

They parted if not friends then at least better acquaintances.

Carol didn't mind chicken. The food was immaterial really. Turkey just made it easy because the leftovers meant she didn't have to cook for a week.

Back in her cozy ninth-floor apartment, she kicked off her shoes, poured herself a chilled Riesling, turned on the TV to watch the news, which always depressed her, but it was a habit to which she had long succumbed. She wished she could break it, tonight of all nights because the ad breaks consisted of promotions for all those Christmas movies of forced good cheer and goodwill to fellow humans.

If I see one more promo for *It's a Fuckin' Wonderful Life*, I'll puke.

It was a pretty wonderful life, she just didn't like the way everybody had to go on and on about it.

The phone rang just after the weather forecast. She'd finished two big glasses of white wine in preparation for the anticipated skirmish. Her mother was reliable as ever. She always waited to see what the temperature was going to be the next day before she rang. It was her Christmas Eve ritual and by the end of the diatribe, Carol's own temperature would have risen considerably.

She tried to keep the sigh out of her voice. "Hello, mum."

Her mother never bothered with pleasantries, believing that as she was paying for a long-distance call she should get straight to the preliminaries.

"You married yet?"

"No, mum." Carol sighed. "Had I made that leap you would have been the first person I contacted."

"You shouldn't be too picky, not at your age. Your biological clock is ticking over fast."

"Yes, mum, I know."

The conversation kept up in much the same tone for another ten minutes or so before her mother ran out of breath and vitriol, finally telling her she should stand up for herself at the company she worked for. "It's not right to keep a daughter from her family on Christmas. It's unchristian. You tell them that."

"I did mum. They said they'll look at letting me have the week off next time."

She'd said that for the past five years but her mother seemed to forget.

"You make sure they do."

When she hung up, Carol knew the words would be the same next year and the year after until she passed forty then references to her biological clock would become moot. She wondered what her mother would find to hoist her with then.

That was one unpleasant call out of the way. Carol only had to survive the minefield that was her sister, Winnie, and then the holiday period was all hers. Winnie loved to ambush Christmas Day when she had enough sauced-up courage to ring. Carol usually let her rabbit on, with the phone on speaker, while she went about her Christmas chores, like preparing her body for the joys of vibrator sex and the fantasy of men-on-men action and a little more men-on-woman action on DVD.

Speaking of which. She went into the bedroom, finding the boxes of goodies at the bottom of her closet. She'd not indulged for some time. The month or so leading up to Christmas was one of her firm's busiest times, what with bonuses and holidays and casuals, and she put in long hours. She used the holiday period to recharge her batteries.

She was tempted to scratch open the packages now but the shiver of anticipation was enough to convince her to leave them until tomorrow. Instead, she stayed so long in her luxurious bath, pampering herself with aromatherapy salts, she had to run the hot water a number of times to up the temperature when it threatened to become too tepid.

She was so mellow when she stepped out of the bath, she was sure her bones had turned to mush. It was almost more than she could manage to stagger to her bed and flop beneath the duvet, drifting off the sleep in expectation of a wonderful Christmas Day.

It started out that way when she awoke from the most refreshing sleep she'd had in an age of Sundays. The day looked forlorn outside her window but she was snug and content. Yes, content. That was a good word to describe her life. It occasionally rose to happy and even less frequently descended to stressed or miserable.

She was pottering along at a steady pace, enjoying what life threw up at her.

It's amazing how quickly Fate can change a person's mind. Carol's wonderful day turned upside down, a little like she did herself when she bounded out of bed full of energy and caught her foot in the bedding, ending up ass over tit on the floor, her foot tangled above her head. Stupidly, she put her arm out to break her fall, now her elbow hurt where she'd bumped it and she was sure there'd be an unsightly bruise in a couple of days.

She picked herself up carefully, checking for sprains or broken bones then examined her body in the full-length mirror looking for abrasions. Still a fine figure of a woman, as they used to say in novels. She fingered her breasts, confident she could stave off the ravages of gravity for a few years yet. Her fingers had a mind of their own, brushing lightly across her slightly curved stomach, past the little field of tufted hair that she kept well-tended, slipping finally into the folds where she truly believed the secrets of the universe lay.

Her fingers were experts, much more so than the stray cock she brought home from time to time when her fingers and the plastic vibrator lost their attraction, but somehow the men never lived up to expectation. They weren't boring exactly in their incessant need to dump a load, or their less than fulsome attention to her needs once they'd come, but they were just a little dull in comparison to what she'd always imagined sex should be.

She didn't believe she was greedy because she wanted more.

If she didn't stop now, though, she would spoil it for later. It took all her willpower to remove her fingers from her pussy, already slick with her juices, to make herself eat a light breakfast and savor that first morning coffee. She looked greedily at the packages neatly wrapped on the settee, awaiting her pleasure.

Circling as if they had a life of their own, instead of just being inanimate objects which she had selected herself, she picked up the first parcel, shivering at what it contained. There was no forcing herself to carefully unwrap the gift; she tore at the paper like a wild animal. No recycling old wrapping paper for her.

The three rented DVD cases sparkled with forbidden treasures, the men on the cover virgins to her sigh, as she ran her fingers over the plastic hoping to feel the muscles and the bulges of the men beneath. She had two men-on-men movies and one men-on-woman, hoping that would be enough to satisfy her cravings for the day. She would take it easy, spread them out, maybe fast forward to her favorite activities if anything got too boring. She had it all mapped out. Life was good.

Turning her attention to the second parcel, her heart beat faster as she tore it open to reveal her sleek new ivory-colored vibrating plastic penis. The color had nothing to do with any racist tendencies, she just didn't fancy the idea of anything pink or blue or green entering her fanny. If she wanted demon sex, she'd join a cult.

The Vibe Mark 2.7x was a thing of beauty. Sleeker, longer and thicker than she was used to. She'd decided to expand her limits this year. Her New Year's resolution would be to experiment, find the interests that would carry her through to a comfortable and satisfying middle age.

Shit! When she flicked the switch at the base of the vibrator there was no familiar buzz, the device lay lifeless in her hands. She unscrewed the mechanism to reveal the tube was empty. She swore so violently the air was in danger of turning blue. Thinking back, she had insisted the adult bookshop assistant where she'd purchased the item, test it before she bought. She was no novice, batteries were never included with things like this, so she'd paid for a set. In her mind's eye, she saw the guy testing the machine, her own satisfaction at the feel of the vibrator, then the batteries being removed so the device didn't accidentally switch on running them flat and fuck, the assistant putting the batteries aside because they didn't fit in the manufacturer's box…

She'd kill that guy behind the counter. He'd been so busy flirting with her; he'd left the batteries out. She'd stuff his balls into her useless plastic tube when she got her hands on him.

All was not lost, she could always use the Vibe Mark 2.7x without the five-speed vibration, after all men's cocks didn't buzz, more's the pity. She remained upbeat and positive. Christmas was a shitty time of year and she commiserated with the millions all over the world who'd already opened their gifts to major disappointment. Hers was minor in comparison.

Looking at the large ivory rocket, she knew she'd need to better lubricate it. It wasn't gigantic but she didn't want to do herself an injury, she wanted to be able to spend the day on her back doing what comes naturally.

She picked up *Men with Muscle*, which would get her primed. She knew there was something wrong as soon as she tugged the disc out of the case: it was crusted with enough dried semen and what looked like pizza cheese she'd need an industrial cleaner to get it off. She shrieked, dropping the disc on the floor, in case it was some form of alien life. Assuring herself it wasn't, she picked it up gingerly between her thumb and forefinger, slipping it back in the case. She'd kill him, the guy at the adult shop.

Think positive.

The second DVD, *Everybody Fucks Raymond*, promised much and delivered nothing. She shook with barely controlled rage as she slid the disc out of her machine within seconds, it being an evangelical tract that someone had substituted for the real movie. So, when she opened the third DVD case and found it empty, she was not surprised. Fate was getting back at her for hating Christmas.

Not thinking rationally, Carol went to her apartment window, hoping, praying, that Mr. Muscles was home in the block across the courtyard and that even a glimpse of his silhouette would be enough to help get her off. No dice. His lights were out. She attempted to push the dildo inside her frustrated pussy but it hurt too much. Not thinking rationally, she flung the sex toy across the room, flinching when she heard it splinter against the wall.

If the assistant from the sex shop had been within twenty feet of her, she would have bitten his head off. Both of them.

She screamed in frustration, wondering whether it could get any worse. It did. The phone rang.

She had no idea who would be ringing this early on Christmas Day.

"What?" she practically yelled down the connection.

"Carol?" a voice asked.

"Who's this?"

"Travis. We met last night over a turkey. Is everything all right?"

"No, it's fucking not," she growled.

"You want I should come over? You know, to chat."

She was being an asshole. Travis was a nice man. "What do you want, Travis?"

"Maybe this is not a good time."

"There ain't gonna be a better time over this whole lousy holiday, Travis, so spit it out now."

"Well, I was just wondering if you'd given any more thought to what I asked yesterday."

No, she hadn't. She'd given him her definite, final, not-gonna-change answer. How many times did she have to tell him? She regretted giving him her number now. She had nightmare visions of him ringing every couple of hours to see if she'd reconsidered. She had to put a stop to that. It would ruin her peace. He'd think she was a bitch but what the hell.

"Travis, there's only one way I'll consent to what you want."

"Name it. We'll do anything."

She giggled in her head and upped the ante. "Okay. Here's the deal. I'll come over and play the perfect girlfriend. In exchange, you let me watch you and Nico doing the dirty tonight after his parents leave."

There was a long pause on the other end of the line. "Just so there's no misunderstanding, you want to watch me and Nico fucking?"

"Uh huh."

"You don't want to join in?"

She wished she'd made that a condition, knowing that would be the killer. But it would also make her seem desperate.

"No, Just watch. Ring me when you and Nico agree, otherwise get off my phone."

God, she was a bitch. Now all she had to endure was her sister. Then she'd have the whole holiday to herself.

If she hadn't left her laptop at work to stop herself from working unpaid during the break, she could have at least downloaded some porn. She was screwed. And not in the good sense. At least on Boxing Day she could get a new toy (*batteries included) and new DVDs. She'd panicked too easily. Sure, everything would be fine; it just meant she'd need to find something to occupy her until tomorrow. One of those tasks she kept putting off, like sorting her hundreds of m/m fantasies according to cock size, gender preference and foreskin over-hang. She almost fell asleep just thinking about it.

Fortunately, the phone rang again. Carol snatched the instrument, a growl of frustration ready in her voice.

"Hello."

"I spoke to Nico and he agreed. As long as there's no touching."

It took Carol's brain a few seconds to work out who the fuck was speaking and what he was talking about. "Look Travis…" She was about to tell him it was all a joke then she remembered she had nothing better to do. Plus, Travis and Nico were hot. It would be better than any porn movie she'd ever watched. She was wet just thinking about it.

"No touching. Except myself."

She heard the hesitation in his voice. "Yeah, that's fine."

"You won't chicken out?"

"I can't say I'm not nervous. I've never done it in front of a woman. Nico's an exhibitionist; I don't dare ask what sort of audiences he's done it for."

She laughed, mainly to relax him but also because she felt something positive had come out of her lousy morning.

"I'll need to bone up on Nico's favorite colors and food and all that shit."

"Why don't I come and pick you up and you can spend the morning with him while I make dinner. We'll be eating early afternoon because his parents are not night people."

They made a time and she gave him her address, mentally calculating how to dress to impress. Though who exactly, she wasn't sure. She smiled to herself when she realized she would not be home to take her sister's call. There was a major break with tradition.

Her behavior was little short of blackmail. What if this escapade got around her gay friends, like Roger? Would they think of her as a scheming bitch? A pervert? Or envy her enterprise?

Wondering if it was too late to call the whole thing off, she managed to keep down some coffee and toast although the butterflies in her stomach threatened to force it back up again. She wanted to feel liberated but instead felt like a dirty old woman. Sure, the guys were only four or five years younger however, she was the one who'd made the impossible demands. But, then again, she was going to see real gay sex in the flesh. The prospect sent anticipation racing through her body setting her core alight with an explosion of sensation.

She wondered how one dressed for such an occasion. She shrugged. Naked would be best. Totally naked or should she be discreetly naked, taking into account the guys' sensibility? Fuck it; they'd be so engrossed in each other they'd probably forget she was even in the room. She liked the idea of being totally naked.

In the end, her choice was a simple outfit that showed enough cleavage that Nico's dad would be envious of his son but not enough that his mother would think her a slut. She was dressing for them, not to impress two gay men.

Pity she couldn't take photos of the action. It was probably too late to add that to her list of demands. Better not to push it, although she wondered if she might take a few happy snaps on her cell phone without getting caught.

She supposed they must think her request was creepy. They had to be desperate to accept. What did she care? All she wanted was to make somebody else's day as miserable as her own.

Travis, when he arrived, refused to co-operate. He was as excited and eager as she was depressed and sullen. What a way to spend Christmas: pretending to be some gay boy's girlfriend to fool his parents, then playing with herself while she watched said gay boy and his partner buggering each other. Assuming they did bugger each other. She couldn't bear it if her misfortune piled even higher and the two guys just jerked each other off. She wished now she'd looked at the fine print more closely. She suddenly realized she had no idea what was expected of her that day.

"You look fabulous," Travis gushed.

How could one stay angry against that?

She thanked him so gracelessly he watched her out of the corner of his eye as he drove off in case she suddenly pulled a knife. He began questioning whether this was such a good idea after all. He avoided turning on the radio in case all that exaggerated cheer and goodwill upset her. Instead, he concentrated on a barrage of small talk to get her mind off what was troubling her, because something obviously was.

He asked several questions hoping that they wouldn't be irritating and she would be drawn in enough to answer. It wasn't a long journey from her apartment to theirs in the gentrified, bohemian quarter. Slowly, she thawed and began asking her own questions. "All will be revealed when you get to our place. Better to hear it from the horse's mouth so to speak," Travis said, relieved she was responding to his attempts to cheer her up.

"And is he hung like a horse?" she asked then blushed, realizing much too late she may have over-stepped the boundaries of what was appropriate even under these strange circumstances.

Fortunately, Travis chuckled. "You'll just have to wait to find out, won't you?"

The apartment was lavish, reeked of success and good taste. Her apartment was splendid enough, but this was superb, and that was before you included the view from the eighth floor window overlooking the river. She murmured her approval as Nico came out of the kitchen drying his hands on a tea towel. He hugged her, kissing her lightly on the cheek.

"Thanks for helping us out," he smiled. He was even more handsome and built than she remembered. A woman could get used to being pressed against that chest, held by those biceps.

"My pleasure," she lied, feeling obliged to add, "I hope you didn't think I was too brazen. It was a bit of a joke really…"

"Not at all," Travis called as he went to check on the turkey, roasting in the oven. "Nico got quite excited, he loves an audience. We had some of the best sex ever last night."

Carol looked stricken. Would they be up to performing again tonight?

"Relax," Travis called. "He's insatiable. Wears me out. He'll be in top form tonight."

"You guys haven't lured me here under false pretenses, have you?"

"Hardly," Nico said. "We're card carrying members of Gays Anonymous. Much too gay for our own good."

Damn.

Over the next hour and a half, Nico and Travis drilled her on the sorts of things she would know as Nico's girlfriend. Travis was designated his flatmate. They'd moved enough of his clothes and other goodies into the spare room that it would look real enough. They'd hidden all the gay porn, anything even remotely gay. It was tedious, but necessary, although Carol could see it rankled with Travis. He was out to his folk and couldn't see why Nico couldn't be the same to his.

The excuse she heard uttered more than once was, "I'm Italian."

He wasn't wrong. Nico's parents, Aldo and Costanza, were old-world Italians, straight out of Hollywood typecasting, and she began to understand his reluctance to come clean. She joined in with the festivities pretending to enjoy it all when she got this funny feeling that she might actually be really enjoying herself, not play acting, although she did have to pretend the superb meal was all her doing. Travis helped her carry it off, of course, as he was the real chef. She hated that he didn't get the credit, because she couldn't cook like this to save her life. The turkey had ended up in a much better home than if she'd 'won' it.

Able to deflect any questions aimed at her, the whole enterprise chugged along flawlessly. When Nico's momma went to the bathroom, after giving the ultimate accolade, "Nico, I'm so glad you find yourself someone who cook almost as good as your momma," the whole party relaxed.

"She can't have got lost," Nico said, after she failed to return for the longest time. "The apartment's not big enough."

"Maybe something has gone wrong in the powder room. I'll go look," Carol volunteered.

She found Nico's momma not in the main bathroom but in the en suite attached to her son's bedroom. She was going through his medicine cabinet.

"You won't find any drugs if that's what you're looking for." Carol could say that with the utmost confidence because she'd searched already.

"Pah," she spat. "I know that. You think a mother can't tell. Show me your hands."

Before Carol could react, Costanza, grabbed her hands and examined them closely, turning them over like some aggressive palm reader.

"You have never cooked a day in your life," she said matter-of-factly.

Carol wasn't sure where this was going but she knew better than to lie to the old woman.

"No, I'm a terrible cook."

"It was this Travis boy who did the cooking?"

"Yes."

"I thought so," she nodded wisely. "You do not live here with my son?"

"No, I have my apartment across town. I like my independence."

"Good," she said. "Whose is the spare bedroom?"

Carol went to say that it belonged to Travis but saw the look Costanza gave her.

"It's spare. For visitors. That sort of thing."

"Or to fool elderly parents if they drop by," she chortled.

"You knew?" Carol asked.

"I guessed. The second bedroom does not have the feel of being lived in. It is not enough to move a few clothes. Anyway, they leave too much evidence in the bathroom. Any mother can read her son by visiting his private bathroom. There are two people living in this room. Two men."

Costanza sat on the large bed, patting the expensive bedspread for Carol to sit beside her. She poured out the whole story while the old woman listened patiently.

"He was scared you would be upset. Family is important to Nico."

"And this Travis boy. What did he think?"

"He wanted Nico to tell you. Nico thought you would be disappointed."

"Disappointed? Pah, I have enough grandchildren from his brothers and sisters, why do I need the aggravation of more? All I care about is that my Nico is happy. His papa feels the same."

Carol helped her up from the bed, taking her arm as they headed back to the dining table.

"Will you tell him you know?" Carol asked.

"No. Let him suffer a bit more for lying to his momma."

The remainder of the afternoon went so well, Carol was sorry when it drew to a close. The funny feeling in her stomach probably went a long way to explaining that. The enormity of what she was about to do hit home with the force of a punch to the solar plexus.

At the door, Costanza turned to the three of them and said, "We enjoyed ourselves so much, didn't we poppa?" He nodded agreement. "We'll be back next Christmas, God willing."

Travis and Nico looked horror stricken while Carol attempted to hide her amusement. Nico's parents were almost out the door when Costanza turned for a final word. "Perhaps next year Carol could join us again. But don't go to a lot of trouble like you did this year. Travis, you leave your clothes in my boy's bedroom. And you take good care of our boy."

She closed the door before anyone could reply.

Travis hooted and jumped into Nico's astonished arms.

They did the washing up in silence, each of them contemplating what was to come. How would it begin? If it was awkward, it would kill the mood but Carol had no clue how to ease them into it. Maybe she should just leave.

Nico begged off finishing the wiping up, leaving the chores to Carol and Travis while he went to the living room. She assumed he was setting up, whatever that entailed. She guessed lubrication, maybe some sex toys. Travis couldn't look at her, obviously embarrassed. She was beginning to feel bad.

Nico came back and took charge. "All right, you two. No putting it off any longer. Travis, go into our bedroom and change. First rule. No clothes in the living room."

Carol was sure she heard Travis gulp before he disappeared down the corridor, then she and Nico went into the living area which now had a much more atmospheric ambience, especially with the subdued lighting. She'd be able to see everything clearly enough without the glaring obviousness of full-on electric light.

Nico had moved an armchair slightly to give it a better view of the divan without making it obvious it was a seat for watching a performance. Nice touch.

She also noticed the lube and a number of hand towels and washers stacked discreetly, ready for use. It seemed a little clinical, albeit practical.

She envied their relationship, wondering what it must be like to be one or the other of them. Travis was obviously nervous and Nico did his best to protect him, to calm his nerves, so much so that Carol felt like total trash. She took the opportunity while Travis was absent to say to Nico, "Look, I never expected it to go this far. I'm sorry. It was meant as a joke. I can see how stressed Travis is. I should go."

"No, a promise is a promise. We Italians always stick to our word. Travis will be all right. I will make sure he does not panic. And in the end it will liberate his soul just a little."

"I don't want either of you to feel cheapened."

Nico looked surprised. "Cheapened? How could that be when we are making love for a beautiful woman to watch? To see how much Travis and me love each other. I think you should go and change in the spare room. By the time you are ready, we will be ready too."

Carol couldn't help it, her heart pounded with excitement. She was really going through with this and, failing Travis chickening out at the last moment, she was going to watch in full flesh color her wildest fantasy. She would have bedded either man gladly had they been straight but the next best thing would be to watch them fuck. She wasn't sure whether she'd be able to hold back from pleasuring herself but as Nico had instructed her to strip, he probably didn't expect her to.

Carol undressed slowly, still unsure whether to flee or not as she would soon be past the point of no return, but when she was naked and felt how wet and eager her pussy was she knew she couldn't back out. Walking slowly down the corridor toward the living room, she heard activity already under way. That there would be no standing around waiting for it to start relieved her greatly. The lack of music was startling; throwing their grunts, moans and crude demands into sharp focus.

She reached the corner and paused hoping to take in the scene before the men spotted her. Nico, naked in all his splendor was indeed an awesome sight, with Travis kneeling between his legs sucking his cock. He *was* hung like a horse, she was pleased to see, between eight and nine inches by her estimation, and thick, although not as thick as the proverbial beer can that most straight guys liked to boast of when comparing the thickness of their cocks: get real guys. If she hadn't been here just to watch, Nico's shaft would have stretched her more than the Vibe Mark 2.7x she had broken apart in her apartment.

Travis had a cock that was almost as large as his lover's, what a mouthful that would make. Carol whimpered softly. Her fingers were already in her pussy, slowly working their way in and out, the tension building. Nico glanced up. She shuddered. Her body reacting instantly to the blatant sensuality of his gaze. The way he looked her up and down showed an appreciation that most gay guys could not fake. He smiled and nodded approval of what he saw then beckoned her into the room.

Travis took cock much farther down his throat than she had ever managed, or thought possible. She marveled at his throat control as he swallowed Nico down to the base. She wondered if he gave lessons.

"That's it, babe, take it all," Nico cooed. "Open up for my cock, Trav. Show Carol how you take cock in that beautiful throat of yours."

He was obviously performing for her. Not that she minded. The view was more exciting close up, so she moved across the room to the armchair and settled herself comfortably, her legs spread wide. Although there was no audience for her, Nico seemed immensely taken with her pussy. She plunged three fingers inside, desperate for relief from the nagging pulse deep inside her core, and matched her thrusts to the rhythm of Travis bobbing up and down on the huge cock between his lips.

She barely had time to get used to the incredible first view of real man-to-man cock sucking when Nico whispered to Travis who stood, squeezing some of the lube on his fingers, using it to grease his ass. Nico watched his boyfriend with admiration. "Bend over, babe, show her what you've got that turns me on so much." Travis obeyed the command; Nico parted his cheeks to press his finger against the hole, before sliding inside.

For the first time in her life she wished she had a strap-on; she'd be up that ass quicker than Errol Flynn.

Nico began directing the action. "Squat over my cock, Trav, slide down my pole so I'm wedged tight inside you.'

Travis squatted, turning his back to Carol. She didn't take it personally, though she would have liked to watch his face while he had that monster plundering his ass. He sank down to Nico's balls without any trouble; obviously used to the feel of that rod inside him. She was envious. Travis began riding Nico's cock like a bronco rider determined not to be thrown from the horse.

"Fuck me Nicky, fuck me hard. Shove your cock inside my hot ass."

"You got it baby." He thrust up as Travis pushed down. "Fuck you're so tight, babe. Milk my cock, milk it."

They were only a few minutes into the activity before Nico looked as if he was about to burst. "Slow down, Trav, I don't want to come just yet. I got something special in mind. Turn around, babe. Let Carol see."

Travis turned then slipped Nico's cock back inside his ass. Now he was facing Carol. It was the first time he'd really looked at her since the fun and games began. She looked like she was on another planet, fingering her pussy like a woman possessed. Travis knew his plan was working, much as it saddened him.

"Look at her pussy, Trav. Doesn't it look juicy, good enough to slam your cock inside?"

Travis wanted to say truthfully that it didn't, but he wasn't about to ruin the fantasy his boyfriend had going on in his head. He concentrated on the awesome feel of Nico's cock sliding in and out of his hot boy pussy, and making his own cock leak.

Nico was holding Travis's cheeks apart so he had deeper access to his boyfriend's cunt, the man cunt he would never tire of fucking. He was watching Carol's reaction. She was so turned on he knew the time was ripe.

"Come over and lick his balls," Travis suggested.

Carol wasn't sure she heard right. She looked at Nico who nodded to her. Travis may have been startled by how quickly events were moving but he was the one encouraging it. Not believing her luck, she slid across the floor to bury her face against Nico's balls, while the hottest guy she knew pushed his prick deep into his boyfriend. The action was so close she could see Travis's ass stretch to accommodate the thick shaft, a shaft she managed to lick surreptitiously as Travis elevated his ass to the head of Nico's cock before plunging back down again.

"You okay, Trav?" Nico asked.

"Uh huh," Travis whispered.

"Why don't you hop off, babe, give Carol a turn?"

Travis flinched. She held her breath for no matter how hard she wanted that cock inside her pussy, she didn't want to break up a relationship. Nico fucked Travis a few more times, then slapped his ass, the indication it was time for a change. Travis seemed to relinquish his spot with the greatest reluctance, but did as instructed. Carol gave him a sympathetic look as she positioned herself over Nico, lowering herself slowly, feeling the head of his beautiful uncut cock push into her. It hurt more than she imagined. She'd never taken a cock so thick before and obviously wasn't prepped sufficiently. She tried a few more times and even though she knew the pain would eventually subside, she felt like she would do herself an injury. To Nico's obvious disappointment, she gave up.

"Go and sit in the armchair, Carol," Travis suggested.

She did as requested, draping her legs over the arms to open herself fully, hoping his plan would work because she wanted that cock badly. "Eat her pussy, Nico. Get her ready to take you."

Nico got down on his hands and knees lapping at her pussy lips like a cat with a bowl of milk, making her writhe with the expert way he used his tongue on her clit, making her wet enough to take ten cocks.

She watched in fascination as Travis lubed Nico's ass while he was distracted then kneeled behind him thrusting brutally into him as if he was punishing his lover for his infidelity.

Travis, despite himself, was turned on watching Nico slurping cunt and was in danger of blowing his load in record time. Trying to ignore the sight before him, he rammed Nico's ass like a piston, the pressure building in his balls, until they threatened to explode. "I can't hold it guys," he warned his playmates, spurring Nico to even more aggressive tongue action. "Yes! Oh fuck!" Carol bucked wildly, shaking from head to toe, Nico tasting her screaming orgasm as Travis squirted deep inside his quivering ass, pulling out when his last drop had been deposited.

Urgently, while Carol was still coming down from her orgasm, Nico kneeled, aimed his cock at her glistening slit, and pushed. It was not the time for niceties so he sank half the length before she pushed her hand against his chest to stop him. Taking deep breaths, she counted to ten then removed her hand so he could bury the remainder of his cock inside her, down to his balls.

"Holy mother of God," Carol yelled, feeling her pussy stretched wider than it ever had been before. Desperate as he must have been to come, Nico still took his time until Carol could accommodate him comfortably. She let him know when she was ready by pushing her pelvis forward to meet him, trying to give him more depth, more feedback that he was doing the right thing.

She didn't expect him to take much notice of her needs, after all she'd already had one orgasm to his zero, but he was driving his cock into her as if daring her not to come again. She looked over to see Travis watching closely, his gaze fixed on Nico's length plunging in and out of her. He was stroking his own depleted cock which was showing every sign of hardening again. Obviously these two could go all night.

Closing her eyes, she attempted to prolong the delicious agony but it was a losing battle. With Nico determined to make her come again, and desperate for his own release it was only a matter of minutes before she groaned and her cunt began to tighten around his shaft as she met and matched his thrusts. Nico upped the pace, his efforts signaled by breathless pants. On the verge of coming, he pulled out of Carol's wet hole to jerk his spunk all over her groin, some of it spattering against her pussy flaps. He flicked the cum off the end of his cock and rubbed the slime on his fingers into her cunt.

"Come on, Trav," Nico encouraged. "Lick it up. Let me see all my hot spunk on your tongue."

Travis hesitated. Nico pushed gently on the back of his head guiding him to the spunk puddling on Carol's groin, close to her excited pussy. Travis's tongue snaked out reluctantly as he had never had sex with a woman, not that he thought slurping up his boyfriend's spunk off her shaved pussy was sex. He sucked the puddles into his mouth, the taste of his lover's sperm galvanizing him. The spunk's familiar taste and texture calmed him. He licked again, his eyes half closed, to avoid looking at her pussy even though ropes of Nico's cum glistened in her folds. He wouldn't go there.

"Hey, baby, this will help you," Nico said, handing his boyfriend the small bottle of liquid.

They didn't use drugs often when it was just the two of them but Nico would sometimes break out the poppers to help Travis relax, get into a scene. It was never more obvious he needed it than now.

Snorting twice in each nostril, he waited for the rush to hit, tasting pussy juices when Nico kissed him tenderly. It was the first time he had tasted cunt.

Nico pulled back. "You like that, Trav? You like the taste, baby? You know I need pussy every now and then."

Travis did know. He could tell Nico was contemplating an attack of pussy lust when the straight DVDs turned up from the video store, followed by Nico coming home later and later at night. He knew Nico was his and if he needed pussy every now and then, he just wished Nico could share it with him like now. He supposed it didn't help that he was one hundred per cent gay, but he could always watch.

Travis's head spun, his heart raced, Nico was telling him to eat up all his spunk. He thought he'd got it all. He wanted to please Nico. There! There were some drops of cum nestled in her pussy lips. Nico pressed his head, closing the gap, so Travis had his mouth up close to Carol's shaved labia.

"Eat it, baby, go on, eat it. That's a good boy," Nico whispered.

He held his breath, hoping the poppers had done the trick. It was so fuckin' hot watching his gay boyfriend with his face close to being buried in wet pussy, he was already hard again. Nico nudged his cock into Travis's already slick hole, gently easing him closer and closer to those pearls of cock juice.

"Lick it up, baby. Lick all my hot juice. Taste it, Trav. Lick it, baby, that's it, lick it all out."

Carol lay back in disbelief that Travis was lapping her pussy. He was no expert but he was still sending shivers through her body. She held his head in place as Nico encouraged, "Suck it, baby, suck it all out. That's the taste on my cock, Trav. You like that taste on my cock? Here baby," he waved the bottle, "Take another hit, maybe that will help you."

Travis withdrew to take mammoth snorts from the little brown bottle. Hoping to please Nico, he plunged at Carol, pushing his tongue vigorously into her slit. She bucked as he entered her.

"Your ass is so hot, babe. I love having my cock inside you." Nico pounded Travis hard, pushing his face into Carol's wet hole at every thrust. Travis became more adventurous, wrapping his lips around her clit, nipping it softly with his teeth, and then running his tongue over the sensitive bud. You can do this, he told himeslf. Silently Travis repeated the mantra over and over. He'd do anything for Nico. That's why he'd invited Carol over in the first place. He didn't give a fuck about Nico's parents but it was a good pretense to get a hot woman to their apartment. He knew Nico's libido would do the rest. When Carol made it a condition that she watch them have sex, it had been an easy step from there to get her involved physically. He just hadn't expected to get this involved himself.

Travis came up for air, his chin shiny with Carol's juices. "Why don't you fuck Carol again, babe. I'm a bit sore," he suggested.

She saw Nico look at him strangely. She guessed Travis had never been too sore in the past but who was she to argue. She wriggled her butt on the settee, moving her legs wider apart in the process, hoping her glistening pussy would be all the invitation Nico needed. He wiped his cock before he kneeled between her thighs, and drilled his hard length into her. She took it easier this time.

Travis called his encouragement, both as an act of bravado and to prove to his lover that he was okay with what he was doing. "Fuck her cunt, Nico. Pound her like you fuck me, babe."

Their roles reversed now: Carol the exhibitionist and Travis the voyeur.

"You look so good back here, Nicky, buried to your balls in her pussy," Travis said.

"You know I gotta have cunt, Trav. Need cunt, love cunt lips wrapped round my prick."

"Go for it, Nicky. You know I'd never stop you. I love seeing your cock buried in cunt, watching you fuck pussy."

"I wanna suck your cock, Trav."

Travis moved quickly around the chair until his cock was level with Nico's face. Bending his legs a little, he jammed his rock hard weapon in his lover's mouth. Carol wasn't sure but she thought she heard Travis whisper, "You owe me big time, Nicky," before the flush of an approaching orgasm swept through her body.

Nico might be mostly gay, but he knew all the ways to bring a woman off with his cock. She looked up at

Travis towering over her, wishing he'd feed her his cock, but she was grateful she got anything at all from him and that he'd deigned to share his magnificent boyfriend, even if it wasn't for totally altruistic motives.

She writhed under the onslaught of Nico's cock until she just couldn't hold off any longer. Her body juddered alarmingly, her muscles clenching around the hard yet silky mass that filled her so completely. "Yes! Oh my God!" Carol shouted her relief as she came for the third time that night. Nico kept pumping her cunt until he too lost the battle and squirted deep inside her already sloppy hole. He fell on top of her, sucking her tits like a baby.

Travis had long since lost the use of Nicky's mouth and was desperate to shoot a second time. He stood over them, jerking his prick, spattering his seed over their faces as they lay exhausted beneath him.

They were all going to need a shower.

There was only slight embarrassment when they eased themselves apart, mainly caused by the unexpected nature of what had occurred. None of them had regrets, least of all Carol who had been invited into Nico and Travis's relationship for the night. She'd learned a lot about herself and her desires from the experience. Her life would never be the same.

"I'll drive her home," Nico volunteered after they'd cleaned up and had a post-prandial coffee. Carol saw the look of distress on Travis's face. He obviously believed Nico would take advantage and attempt to make another date to hook up without him. She didn't want that. Sure, she'd had fun but she didn't want to interfere on a regular basis. "Where do you live?"

"She lives in the same complex as Dallas, on the other side of the courtyard," Travis said.

"Who's Dallas?" she asked in an effort to avoid a confrontation between the two men.

"He's a gym bunny we see from time to time. Even bigger muscles than Nico's," Travis said.

"No, they're not," Nico sulked, showing off his bicep so that Carol drooled, almost tempted to take him up on his offer of a lift so she could get in a little Christmas car sex. Better not.

She wondered whether they were talking about her Mr. Muscles so she described her man to them. Her heart sank when they agreed that was Dallas.

"Shit." That was depressing news.

"What's the matter?" Travis asked.

"I've been fantasizing about him for months. Now I find out he's gay."

Nico laughed. "He's about as many parts gay as I am straight. Just gets the urge for cock occasionally and we're more than happy to oblige."

"How big…?" Carol felt tawdry asking such a question but she couldn't help herself.

Travis nodded in Nico's direction. "About the same as…"

Carol's mouth watered and her body heated with desire at the thought of making out with him.

"I just wish he'd leave his blinds up when he exercises so I can get better eye candy while I–"

"Too much information," Travis said, placing his hands over his ears.

"About that lift?" Nico said hopefully.

"Thanks, but I've got friends in the neighborhood and I told them I might drop in Christmas night."

She could see Travis knew that was a lie, smiling his appreciation for her consideration. It also told her in no uncertain terms that while he knew he'd made the right decision for Nico he didn't want it to become a habit. She was fine with that. She left, promising to keep in touch. That may have been a lie, although she was likely to run into them at various functions around town. As she flagged down a lone taxi prowling the late Christmas streets, she was amazed at how her initially disastrous day had turned out. She'd send a prayer of thanks to the Fates once she figured out which one was responsible.

Tired, eager to spend the next day or so recovering from one of the most intense sexual episodes of her life, she realized neither of them had kissed her. Perhaps an act too far. It had been sex, not love. Some people didn't get the difference. Still, she had enough visualization material to last her for a very long time indeed.

As she entered her apartment, weary and hungry, thankful Travis had given her a container of leftovers that would last a day or two, she noticed the light was on in Mr. Muscle's…Dallas's apartment. She went to her window, staring across the expanse that divided them, seeing his body silhouetted against the light. Suddenly, the blind raised and Dallas was staring straight at her, a phone cradled against his ear.

She thought of quickly hiding but that would be more embarrassing than being caught staring. He continued to look straight at her as he chatted on the phone. She wondered whether it was Travis he was talking to and that's why he'd pulled up the blind. She had her answer when his hand went to his crotch, squeezing it suggestively. Then he waved.

CHRISTMAS ON THE ROCKS

Barry Lowe

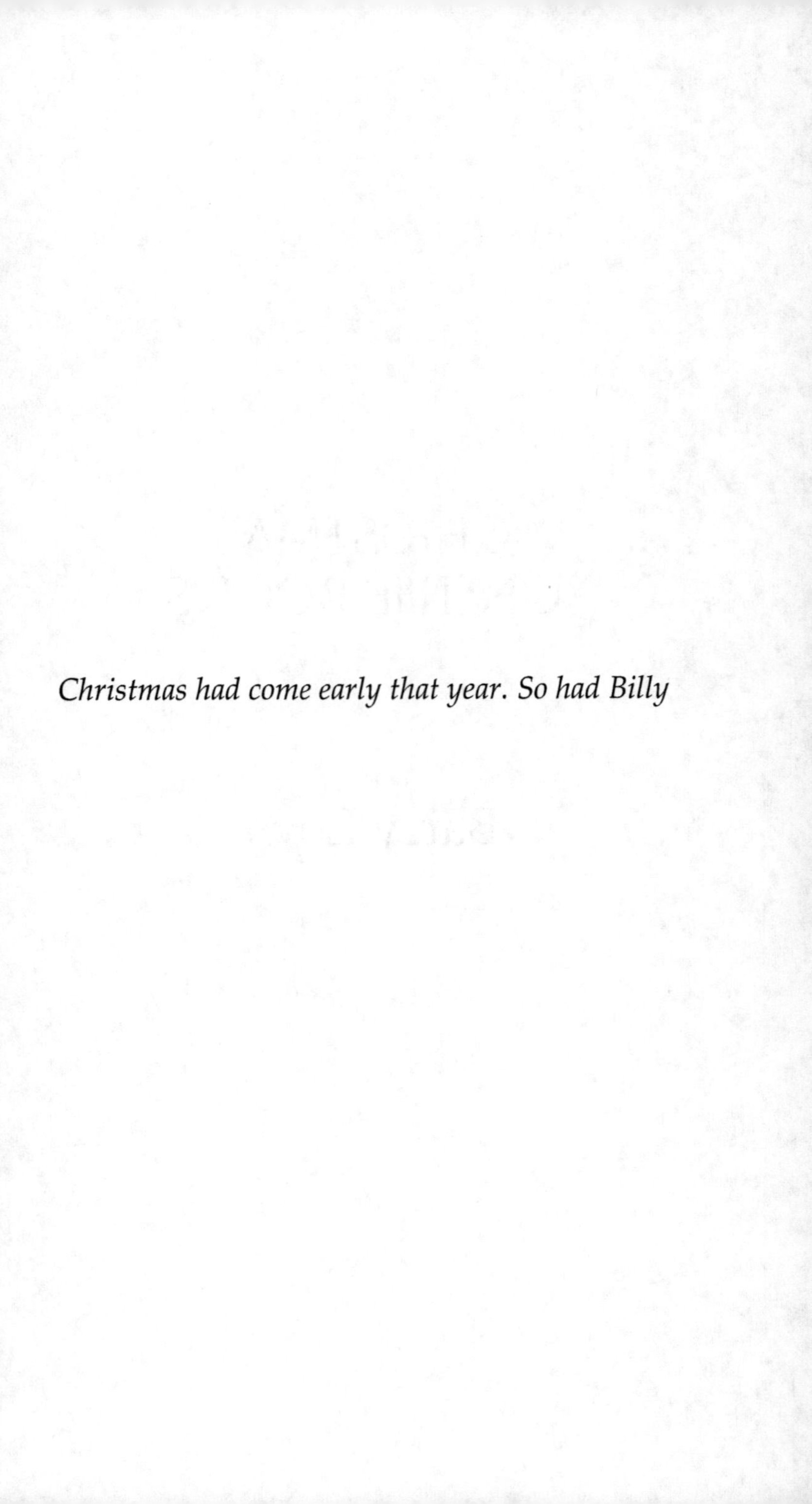

Christmas had come early that year. So had Billy

Billy gets really frisky around Christmas. It takes all my strength to keep him in check. He has the sort of personality that's prone to over-indulge in recreational substances and booze, particularly if forced on him by a second party, and that, in turn, leads to an abundant over-indulgence in Billy's favorite party-time recreation: sex. Billy can be, given the right circumstances, a slut.

It starts in September, the southern hemisphere spring. His libido is lethargic during the winter, he almost hibernates but as soon as the sun goes from watery warmth to slightly sizzling it's off with the shirts and the jumpers and on with the T-shirts, singlets and very tight shorts. He is continually horny, like he comes on heat. You can set your seasonal clock to his sexual behavior. Most of the time he keeps it in check, merely exhibiting himself and his availability. Fortunately, I've got what it takes between my legs although it's a roller coaster ride trying to keep up.

It doesn't happen often but when he does break out, courtesy of the aforementioned libido enhancing drugs or booze, or some perceived slight from me – let's face it, just about anything sets him off when he gets that 'itch' – it takes all my strength of character and my trampled pride to indulge him, rescue him, and take him back home. I love the silly bugger, that's my only excuse.

This particular Christmas was going to be a lousy one. We were pretty broke, not an uncommon occurrence, the mortgage was getting behind, I was worried sick, and Billy's part-time kitchen work was drying up when we least expected it. Firms were economizing on Christmas parties. I was working as much overtime as possible so I was getting home too buggered to bugger Billy who was becoming friskier by the day. I knew the signs, but I also knew that a perfunctory fuck would not satisfy him any more than the rubber dildos he used regularly on his own ass when I was not home.

He's not totally insensitive and realized my worry over apartment repayments as well as ongoing expenses was playing havoc with my sexual appetite and my ability to please him. But I didn't want to burden him with things beyond his control. For his peace of mind I kept most of the bad news from him, sharing only the good. There was blessed little of that at the time. I decided we'd sit down and have 'the talk' about finances in the New Year, and the very real option of selling up and downsizing. Let him enjoy the holiday period.

Meanwhile, I just had to endure his constant harping on my lack of sexual enthusiasm, my reluctance to go out partying, my near permanent total exhaustion, and my lack of interest in anything at all he was interested in. After another of his particularly self-indulgent and whiny attacks on my worth as a lover, I'm afraid I'd had about as much as I could stand. Okay, so it was my fault for not taking him into my confidence, and I would probably do things differently given my life over again and knowing what I know now, but he pushed me too far. He knew how to press my buttons. He screamed at me after I'd turned him down again about going to a show that would cost two days' pay. "You're no fuckin' fun at all anymore. Maybe I should have stayed with Jerry."

The silence that followed was deafening. Jerry, after all, was my former butt ugly boss, who had not only had his way with Billy in front of me once, but had also managed to steal Billy away from me for a number of months until he got tired of him and passed him on to another couple who seriously abused his trust. As a result, Billy had a tattoo which read 100% Pure Slut on his butt. It was only with a great deal of public humiliation, patience, and ingenuity that I managed to win him back. Now he was throwing it in my face.

He must have known he'd gone too far, his look of regret said as much, but he was damned if he would apologize. It was not in his nature. And it was not in my nature to hit him, or walk away and slam the door. No, I had to be sarcastic.

I went to the bureau drawer and scribbled a phone number on a Post-It! note and handed it to him. "Here. That's the last known phone number for your pal Jerry. If he's not there, I'm sure they'll pass on a message. Maybe he can pay you again so we can get out of this hideous financial mess we're in. The apartment's in the balance."

Then I walked off and slammed the door. Only later, I thought perhaps I could have phrased it better.

Normally when we have a quarrel, one or the other of us climbs into bed and apologizes with a kiss and a cuddle rather than let the argument stew. Not that night. Billy slept in the spare bedroom. And the next night. And from then on. We were civil to each other but we ate our meals separately. Billy kept out of my way when I was getting ready for work and when I came home late at night exhausted.

Our blowup spurred him on to seek a job – any job. I found pages of the local job market classifieds circled but he obviously had had little luck as they also had a large cross through them. He was always in bed, in the guest room, every morning when I left for work. I would tiptoe in, arrange the sheet and blanket around him, and peck him lightly on the forehead or the cheek, before leaving quietly.

As September rolled into October, the unexpected occurred. One night I came back from work and Billy was ironing a waistcoat in the living room while watching television. He looked like his old self again, and the smell of warm food wafted from the kitchen. He welcomed me home by flinging his arms around me and giving me a wet, sloppy kiss and a quick grope. He sat me down and served me dinner, playing the attentive lover, to the extent he gave me a tasty blow job as I sat watching TV to unwind. I should have known he was buttering me up.

He was so eager with his news, he jumped to his feet while he was still swallowing the load I'd dumped in his mouth, wiped his lips with the back of his hand, and danced about the room. "I've got a job! I've got a job!"

"That's wonderful news," I cheered.

"It's only for a month or two in the lead-up to Christmas, but I'll be able to help with the phone bill and the power."

"You don't have to do that," I said, but secretly glad he would be bringing in a little extra cash. It all helped. "What sort of job is it?"

He suddenly looked embarrassed, like he'd oversold his prospects. "I get to wear a uniform. You stay right there and I'll show you."

I had no trouble following orders, I was too exhausted to move, especially after a Billy Oral Special. That was another of the problems I had with Billy when he became uncontrollable sexually. He had a reputation. No, not in the bad sense. Well, not in any way that I would consider bad. He was known to be one of the best fucks in the city. Especially if you got him in the right mood, and there were plenty of people out there who wanted to get him in the right mood because he was one of the cutest little blond fuckers you ever laid eyes on. And he worked out in the gym to keep his body as taut and terrific as any top model, although it was his ass that was his salient feature. Correction: as superb as his butt was, it was actually his asshole that was the source of his fame.

While he was changing into his new working clothes he chatted from the bedroom. "With my skills, or should I say my almost complete lack of, there wasn't much going so don't get disappointed and give me that lecture on holding out for something commensurate with my abilities. No one's hiring in that field." Billy was an unemployed sous chef. "Close your eyes. Go on, close them. Are they closed?"

"Yeah," I called.

I heard activity as Billy obviously got himself in position to pose.

"Open them. Ta da!" He threw his arms in the air as if he were a Broadway diva, although in the outfit he was wearing he looked more like a sleazy 42nd Street stripper before the neo-moralists moved in to clean up the area.

I had steeled myself against every contingency I could think of. Except the one that confronted me. I smiled weakly as I looked at Billy, practically naked, eagerly awaiting my approval. He twirled on the spot as if his uniform was something that would not be out of place on the Oscar's Red Carpet. It was more likely to get him arrested.

"Billy, I can practically see your asshole when you turn around."

"Yeah," he said patting his butt. "They said they'll get me a better fit once I start. They just loaned me this so I could get used to wearing it. And could get some practice in."

"What's to get used to?" I asked, a tinge of sarcasm creeping in. "You're wearing a bright orange cap, a waistcoat, a pair of the tightest vibrant orange shorts I've ever seen and which will strangle all the sperm in your balls if you don't get out of them soon, and a pair of orange sneakers."

"Tandoori," he said, with a touch of disappointment in his voice.

"What?"

"It's tandoori, not orange."

I had to salvage his pride. "I bet you'll be the sexiest pizza delivery boy in the country."

"You think?" he said, perking up a little.

"I didn't think they employed men for the job," I said.

"They don't. I'm the first. The only. It's a test run. The company is interested in tapping the gay market."

In that outfit the gay market would be mighty interested in tapping Billy.

Every fiber of my being wanted to scream, 'You'll take this job over my dead body,' but I had to be supportive. The distinctive orange, excuse me, tandoori outfit was normally the domain of a voluptuous female, usually just over the right side of the age of consent, and who didn't mind showing off as much of her body in public as legally permissible while flirting outrageously with male customers. It was rumored, some of the girls, particularly college students, were not averse to allowing a little feel of their perky tits, sometimes allowing further liberties if the tip was large enough. It was all hearsay. What wasn't in doubt is that Pizza with Everything was run by Billy's uncle, Ram, his nickname supposedly because of what he had hanging between his legs. He was the black sheep of Billy's family. He'd married a former porn star, twenty years his junior, and made no secret of his prodigious appetite, not only for pizza, but for the nubile young women who worked for him.

"What exactly do you have to do in this job?" I asked casually.

"Hey, don't worry, love." Billy came and sat on my knee to give me a reassuring cuddle. "It's nothing like that. I may flirt a little to get a bigger tip but I won't be delivering anything that isn't on the menu."

Billy finds it almost impossible to lie. He gives himself away when he's guilty but I didn't notice any tell-tale signs as he explained his job. Still, he may not intend straying from the menu but there would be some guys out there who would be trying everything to ensure he did. Hell, he didn't need a job as a pizza delivery boy to come across those temptations.

"When do you start?" I asked, giving his new job my imprimatur.

Billy showered me with kisses. "Tomorrow. The only bugger is that I'll be at work when you get home at night. The job starts at 5pm until last orders. We won't get to see a lot of each other over the next few weeks but it will make Christmas better, won't it, Steve?"

Billy was so eager for validation I made all the right noises. When he got tired of prancing around in his ultra-revealing outfit, he led me to the bedroom and I leisurely put his marble-hard butt and its warm inviting hole to good use, reminding myself that I was the incredibly lucky boyfriend of the hottest ass in the country.

When we were lying arm in arm after we'd both dumped a load, I nuzzled Billy's neck and gave him the good news. "With you earning an income we can afford to have our usual Christmas party," I announced triumphantly.

I expected squeals of delight but all I got was silence.

"I thought you'd be pleased," I said.

"What's say we skip the party and put the money toward paying bills?"

Something was up, apart from my good self, because Billy had never been practical with money before.

"I thought our Christmas party was the highlight of the year." I was slightly miffed at his seeming display of ingratitude.

"Uh, no, not really," he mumbled.

"What do you mean, not really?"

"Here we go," he sighed. "I was hoping to avoid this argument."

"There won't be an argument," I lied. "I just want to know why you've suddenly turned against the party."

"It's not the party as such." He was choosing his words carefully. "It's the people who come to them."

"They're all our closest friends," I said.

"Your closest friends."

"My friends are your friends."

"Nah, your friends are sleazy scumbags who are all trying to fuck me behind your back and trying to get me to move in with them." I saw him tense, waiting for the verbal onslaught.

The idea was so ludicrous, I laughed.

"I know you're hot, Billy. And your reputation is all over the state, but my friends wouldn't do that."

He shrugged like he didn't want to argue the point. "Okay, have it your way. But there is maybe one or two of your closest mates who haven't seriously tried it on with me when you're not looking or you're not home and who haven't offered me money, an overseas holiday, whatever I want, to move in with them."

"I bet you wouldn't say that again to their face."

"I bet I would," he said and rolled over in the bed.

"If it's true, and I say 'if', why haven't you told me before?"

"I didn't want to upset you."

I snapped. I couldn't help myself. "Well, if you didn't dress like a slut and give everyone the 'come on, fuck me' routine—"

He smiled sweetly. "I thought you liked to watch me make a slut of myself. I thought it turned you on."

"The problem with you, Billy, is you have no self-control. You have no discernment when it comes to who you flirt with. Even worse, who you...play with."

"I thought that's what being a slut was all about."

"Not with my friends!"

"They're not friends. I've tried to tell you for years. They're sleazebags who hang around you in the hope of sinking their cocks into me."

We were back to where we started.

He got out of bed, grabbing his pillow. "I think it best if I sleep in the spare bedroom permanently." Our rapprochement had been short-lived.

I could not bring myself to ask him to stay. I'd upset him, not least by calling him a slut, the term of abuse that others used when they were trying to humiliate him. I lay awake for hours mulling over what he'd said. I couldn't bear to believe that most of my friends and, yes, I had to agree they were my friends, not his, would behave so crassly toward him. I fell asleep wondering.

The next week was painful. We barely spoke to each other. His excuse was that he didn't want to disturb me when he came in late and didn't want me to disturb his sleep when I got up in the morning. But I'd lie awake until all hours waiting for his familiar sounds and smells before I could fall asleep. Only once did I try to cajole him back into our bedroom. I'd kissed him and tasted the spice of another man's spunk on his lips and tongue and had recoiled. That put paid to our reconciliation. My look of shock must have registered more disapproval than I had felt. Billy's exile continued: my torment made a thousand times worse by my imagination.

My work was suffering, I couldn't sleep, and I was an accident waiting to happen. I had to get help. I decided to seek the advice of two of my closest friends, Murray and Dale. They'd had similar ups and downs in their long-term relationship, and I'd helped them through those times, mainly by the example of Billy's and my rock solid commitment.

I drove over to their place one night after Billy had left for work. He would detest that I'd brought other people into our problems, but I had nowhere else to turn as Billy would not talk to me, always pleading that he was 'too exhausted.' Dale made me a stiff drink when he saw how upset I was. "We were about to eat, do you want to join us?" he asked.

"If I'm not intruding."

"After all you've done for us, it would be a pleasure," Murray said.

"Trouble at home?" I did not like the snarky tone to Dale's voice. Billy's accusations were poisoning me and made me suspicious of everyone and their motives.

"That's what I came to talk about."

Murray put his arm around my shoulder in comfort as Dale handed me my bourbon and ice. I gulped the first mouthful, requiring the courage of alcohol to confess that my perfect relationship was anything but. Dale refilled my glass to better lubricate my tongue. I was about to launch into my tale of woe, when there was a knock at the door.

"That'll be the pizza," Murray said smiling.

"That will cheer you up," Dale said.

"Nothing like a bit of eye candy with your hot meal." Murray was positively slobbering.

"You invited me to stay for pizza?"

"It's pizza night, we have pizza every Wednesday night."

I begged off joining them. "I think I'd better go."

"Stay a minute." Murray was trying to be supportive but he was making things much more difficult. "Steve, this guy is supposed to be amazing. Delivers the pizza and does anything at all you want and more. He's supposed to be the hottest thing on two legs. Everyone we know says he's worth every cent, though the pizzas don't come cheap."

There was no reason to believe it was Billy at the door but my head told me otherwise. Murray and Dale obviously had no idea as to the identity of the pizza delivery boy or else were consummate actors. I knew they weren't after attending their diabolically bad performances in an amateur all-male production of *The Women* the year before.

"Is there another way out?"

"Not unless you climb out the window," Dale said.

"I'm begging you. As a friend. Don't tell him I'm here."

"Don't tell who?" Murray seemed genuinely baffled.

"The pizza boy."

"Why? Are you having it off with him? Are you on a low carb diet and you're scared he might tell..."

The look of horror on my face must have given the game away.

"Oh. My. God." Dale could scarcely conceal the glee in his voice.

Murray was less obvious. "The pizza delivery boy is Billy?"

"Did you order from Pizza with Everything?"

Murray nodded his head.

My heart sank. "It could be Billy. Please don't tell him I'm here. He'll think I'm checking up on him."

"Why would he think that? We're friends after all." I couldn't detect any sarcasm in Murray's question.

"He's been rather secretive about his job lately and that's caused a bit of friction." I thought that half-truth would satisfy them.

Murray was all sympathy. "You think he's delivering a bit more than pizza?"

My face said it all.

"We heard this pizza boy puts out," Dale said.

"Not that we were interested in that. But his ass is supposed to be something special. And Dale was getting a little jealous every time someone mentioned it."

"So it's not likely to be Billy," Dale was vicious when he got started.

The knock was more insistent this time.

I pleaded. "Please don't tell him."

Murray's reply was less than convincing. "Uh, okay."

Dale crossed his heart but looked rather smug about it.

"Just in there," Murray said, pointing to the walk-in closet near the door. "You'll be able to see and hear everything without being seen yourself."

"When he's gone I think you'd better come out and tell us the whole story," Murray said.

I ducked into the coat closet near the front door which had a ventilation hole at eye height and a great view of the living area.

Dale opened the door and snickered. "Hey, Billy. How are you, mate? Come in."

He draped his arm over Billy's shoulder in a much-too-familiar manner considering he purported not to like him. Or was he doing this for my benefit? Surely Billy would deliver the pizza, collect his money and go. He only ever expressed intense dislike of these too.

"Hey, Billy," Murray called. "Since when you been delivering pizza?"

"A few weeks now."

"You like the job?"

"Love it. I meet such interesting people."

"Pay good?" Dale asked. He'd always been mercenary.

"Oh, it's okay. I can make up for it with tips though."

Murray kept drawing him out. "Looking hot in that outfit, Billy. It doesn't leave much to the imagination."

"That's the whole point, I guess. The customers seem to like it."

"You must get hit on a lot."

Billy smiled. "Yeah."

"You know how to handle yourself if the buyers get too rough?"

Murray was a good mate. He was asking all the right questions. All the things he knew I couldn't ask without Billy thinking I was checking up on him.

"No one ever gets too rough for me." Billy never knew when to stop. I knew he was only being friendly because the job dictated it but there was a limit to revealing confidences.

"Let me see, you ordered the Spicy with Double Topping?"

"That's it."

"Uh," Billy hesitated. "You guys still want to go ahead now you know it's me?"

"Why wouldn't we?"

"I thought you guys didn't like me."

"We don't have to like you to do this," Dale said, running his hand over Billy's tight ass. "Aw, shit, Murray, feel this."

Murray squeezed Billy's butt and moaned his satisfaction.

"You up for it?" Murray asked.

"Sure," he smiled.

"Even though it's us?"

"That makes it even better," Billy said and pulled his vest open to reveal his six-pack and his rock hard pecs.

"I've fancied you guys ever since we were introduced."

"Fuck," Dale panted. "We've wanted to fuck your hot ass since forever, but Steve's so jealous he wouldn't let us near you."

"Think how fuckin' hot it will be now then."

"Will you tell him?" Dale asked.

"Fuck, no! Will you?"

"So he doesn't know you're doing this?" Murray was suspicious, and glanced toward where I was hiding. "This is not some sort of set-up?"

"No way. He knows I deliver pizza. That's all."

"What if he did know?" Murray was conflicted between me, his best friend watching the activity from my hiding place, and Dale's all-out assault on Billy that was happening in front of him, obviously uncaring about my feelings.

"Fuck him," Billy said. "It's my body."

"Cool," Dale said stripping Billy's shorts off. "Bend over, slut."

Billy, naked and already hard, bent over and grabbed his ankles. Dale kneeled and parted his cheeks, fingering his asshole. "He's all yours Murray." They were probably eager to begin in case I tried to put a stop to the activity.

I wasn't going to do that. Not yet, at any rate. I wanted to see how far my erstwhile friends would go. And I wanted to see just what sort of pizza delivery boy Billy really was. It looked as if he was every gay man's wet dream come true.

Dale had stripped off his clothes, his leaking cock looking mean and spiteful. With a scream of "Suck it, mongrel cunt whore," Dale slammed it into Billy's mouth choking him. Murray watched in awe as his boyfriend attacked mine. Billy opened his throat and Dale just slammed in and out until his cock was covered in puke and drool, the sounds of deep penetration gagging echoing around the living room. The ramrod face fuck kept up for a good five minutes until Dale relaxed and let Billy catch his breath.

"Fuck, Dale. I've never had my throat pounded so good. You like feeding it to me, huh? Watching it slide down my throat. Go on; choke me on your big hot cock. Steve never feeds me enough cock, that's why I gotta get it outside."

Murray was still watching the action, playing with his own prick that seemed eager to get at Billy's ass.

He must have been nervous because he kept glancing my way. The decision was taken out of his hands when Billy backed up, grabbed his cock, guiding it into his hole.

"What about Steve? I'm his best friend" Murray squeaked.

Billy sighed as he impaled himself right down to Murray's balls. "Don't give me that shit. You don't like Steve."

"Nah, never did like the fucker!" Dale agreed, watching his lover penetrate deep into Billy's butthole.

"Steve won't let me fuck his friends."

"Why not?" Dale asked.

"Too scared they'll be better than him, I guess."

"And are we better than him, Billy?" Dale asked.

"Fuck, yeah, do you even have to ask?" Billy grunted as Murray picked up the pace.

"You are so fuckin' nasty, Billy," Dale sat in an armchair watching the action and, behind that, my hiding spot. He was slowly jerking his cock with the remnants of Billy's puke. He was letting Billy run off at the mouth because he knew every word was a stab straight to my guts. "How many guys you had so far tonight?"

"Eight. You guys are the last order."

"Fuck, you're still so tight," Murray said. "Your ass in unbelievable."

"They don't all want to fuck me. Some want to watch me strip or suck me off. Some want me to be really nasty." He left the idea hanging.

"Are you a nasty whore, Billy?" Dale probed.

"You bet I am."

"A filthy cum-sucking slut?"

"That's me."

Nothing Dale said phased Billy. I hoped he wasn't leading him into a trap.

Murray was gasping. "Fuck, oh fuck. This is the best ass I have ever screwed! No wonder Steve doesn't want to share you."

Billy encouraged him. "Come on, Murray. Slam your cock into me. I want that hot hard cock of yours squirting spunk deep inside me. Then I'll lick you clean. That's it Murray, your cock feels so fuckin' good."

His voice was low and hypnotic and Murray was close. Billy got that look on his face when he's concentrating all his energy on his butthole, squeezing it like a suction cup around the invading prick.

Murray let out a strangulated scream. "Holy mother of god. I can't take any more." He humped against Billy's butt five or six times and collapsed on his back. He caught his breath and pulled free, spunk dribbling down Billy's leg, before pushing the slimy cock in Billy's mouth for a spit clean and polish. Then, still breathing heavily, he swapped places with Dale and sank exhausted into the chair.

Dale lay Billy on the rug and pushed his legs over his shoulders. Then, without any preliminaries, sank his cock right into Billy's guts, the previous spunk deposited there acting as lube. Dale wrapped his hand around Billy's throat, choking his head in position so they had to look each other in the eye. I could see Billy grit his teeth as he stared into the black eyes of his defiler. "Do your worst fucker," he hissed.

Ramming his cock into Billy, Dale rotated his hips to enter from a different angle each time, varying his thrusts to keep the man speared by his prick on the alert. Billy groaned which meant the fucker was getting to him. Dale was a magnificent animal and it was almost a pleasure to watch him plowing my far from defenseless boyfriend. I was hard. I undid my fly and dragged out my cock to gently apply pressure to the already leaking piss slit.

"Who's the best you've had tonight, Billy?"

"Fuck, no contest. You two. You both make me so fuckin' horny. I need your cocks inside me. I've needed them since that first time I met you. I wanted you to throw me down and fuck me right there and then."

"You're not just saying that, Billy?" Dale was no dummy.

"Fuck, no. I mean it. You guys are the hottest fuckers I ever met. Your cocks are just perfect for my cunt holes. You notice that way my ass muscle gripped when you were fucking me?" Both men agreed they had. "That was special just for you guys. It drives Steve wild. I promised him he would be the only guy I ever did it to."

"Shit, eh," Murray laughed.

Dale goaded. "What else will you do Billy that Steve wouldn't want you to?"

"Anything. Especially if it's real nasty."

Dale picked up pace, his body slapping loudly against Billy's butt. "You. Are. My. Kind. Of. Slut. Boy." Dale was obviously dumping a load inside my lover.

He pulled out and Billy slumped on the carpet, his ass in my direct line of sight.

Dale pulled him up on his knees, doggy style. "Show us your ass, Billy. Let's see the spunk we blew up that cum dump ass of yours."

Billy reached back to spread his cheeks, and cum dribbled out of his butt hole. Dale held a glass that he'd picked up from the kitchen, under the puffy ass lips. "Here, Billy. Push out the loads inside you."

Billy squeezed his ass, wads of cum drooling into the glass.

"How many loads, Billy?"

"Five. Plus your two."

"Fuckin' nasty!"

"Anything for you guys."

"Would you tell that to Steve if he was here now," Murray asked.

"Fuck, yeah."

"What would you tell him, Billy?" Dale asked.

"You guys know how to treat a cum dump slut."

Dale grabbed him hard again by the throat. "Say it louder, Billy!"

"Steve fucks like a girl," Billy shouted. "I need man cock like you guys."

"And you're not lying, Billy?"

"I'll show you how much I mean it. I'll stay for another session with you two off the clock, my treat. You can do whatever you want."

"What if we want to fuck you in front of Steve to teach him a lesson that he's got to share you?"

"I'd love that," Billy's mind was probably racing into the fantasy.

"What if we want our friends to fuck you?" Murray said.

"Bring them on."

Dale handed Billy the glass of slime. Billy raised it and said, "Skol. Here's to you guys, and loads more man cream." He tipped the glass and we watched fascinated as his throat muscles bobbed, swallowing the juice, gagging only once but keeping it down.

Dale was all admiration. "Fuck, that was hot."

Murray slapped Billy's face with his hard prick before sliding it between his lips, holding the back of his head obviously enjoying the warmth of Billy's slime-slicked throat. I watched Murray lean over, hooking his thumbs into Billy's sphincter, pulling it open.

"Fuck, that ass is so sweet, I bet everyone wants to fuck it," Murray said.

"You'd let them fuck it, too, wouldn't you, Billy?"

"Hell, yeah. I want to take every cock in the world."

"What's your hottest fantasy right now, Billy? If Steve was here to watch."

Billy groaned. "Shit, that's my dream. Get all Steve's friends who he thinks are so fuckin' cool, they all try to fuck me when he's not looking. Get them in one room."

"What then, Billy?"

"Get Steve over and make him watch every one of his so-called friends fuck my ass until I'm full of their spunk. Then make him suck it out, taste the slime they've been waiting to pump into me behind his back for years."

"Off the clock?"

"Yeah, I promised."

"Give us the names, Billy," Murray said.

"You guys are serious?" Billy asked.

"Deadly."

Billy looked like the cat that got the cream as he rattled off the names of my closest friends. Eight in all. Mates who I thought were on my side. This would prove it one way or the other. One by one Dale dialed their numbers on Billy's mobile and invited them over to meet the famed pizza delivery boy that everyone was talking about. He didn't let on the delivery boy's identity. Two weren't home and one wanted to bring his boyfriend.

I should have put a stop to it, but I wanted to see who of my friends would stand up for me. Murray and Dale were counting on that to stop me from interrupting their game plan.

"Some of them should be here in about ten to fifteen minutes. Those that live further away could be up to half an hour," Murray said as he went into the kitchen to put on a pot of coffee. He and Dale had slipped on shorts but insisted Billy remain naked, a state of dress he loved.

"You really up for this?" Murray asked.

"You don't have to keep asking," Billy said, slightly annoyed. "If I wasn't, I wouldn't be here."

"I gotta say, Billy, that ass of yours is the best I've ever had. You're sitting on a fortune," Dale said,

Billy smirked. "Yeah, a lot of guys have told me that."

"You ever think of leaving Steve?" Dale asked.

"Why? You offering?"

Dale looked to Murray who nodded his head almost imperceptibly. "Maybe."

"You think you got what it takes to look after me? Satisfy my asshole?"

"Didn't you say we were the best?" Murray asked.

"Yeah, I did, didn't I?"

"Well?" Dale demanded.

"You'd let me fuck other guys? Fuck your friends?"

"Fuck, no!" Dale was adamant.

Billy shrugged that the conversation was over.

"Steve doesn't let you fuck his friends either," Murray pointed out.

Billy smiled. "But I do anyway."

Dale was so confident in his ability to satisfy Billy. "We'd keep you too busy. You wouldn't have the time."

"If you say so." Billy sounded bored. "You gonna invite Steve to the party?"

I held my breath. I didn't want my hiding place revealed because Billy would still think I was checking up on him and I wanted to see how true my closest friends were or whether they were turncoats like Dale and Murray.

Murray and Dale exchanged looks.

"I rang," Murray said. "No answer. I left a voicemail message. But I'll try him again once everyone arrives."

"You really want him to witness you being a fuck slut for all his closest friends?" Dale was trying to get his head around the idea. "You must really hate him."

"Nah, you don't understand."

Murray was curious. "What do you think he'll do if he catches you?"

"He could throw me out in the street." Billy seemed awfully calm about the prospect. "Or he can accept it, no questions asked."

"What, public humiliation? In front of his best friends? All fucking his lover?" Murray was incredulous at the prospect.

I began to think they'd forgotten I was in the closet listening to every word until there was a knock at the door and on his way to answer it, Dale distracted Billy's attention and Murray slipped me a cup of coffee. There's a lot to be said for civilized gay male behavior. They might have been cuckolding me by buggering my boyfriend in front of me but they remembered the social niceties. That goes a long way in my book. But not nearly far enough to make up for what they were doing. I didn't know whether they thought my non-intervention was passive acquiescence in their activity or whether I was just some poor cuckold who would tolerate his boyfriend's flagrant infidelity in a desperate attempt to keep him. They would be wrong on both counts.

The first to arrive was Kyle, who'd stopped off to pick up Jason, both guys who I went bar hopping with in my bachelor days. They heartily approved of Billy and had given no indication of having designs on his body. Kyle barged into the living room. "Lead me to him. I've heard so much about this pizza delivery guy I have to see him with my own eyes before I'll believe it."

"Hi Murray, Hi Billy," he called while he looked around. "Where is he? Don't tell me you've got him in the bedroom already? You cunning deviants!"

Dale smirked. "No, he's here in the room with us."

Jason looked about confused.

Billy drew his legs up on the lounge and parted them. A sly grin crept across Kyle's face. "Oh sweet Jesus. Tell me you're fuckin' serious, dude. Tell me I'm not dreaming."

Dale was as proud as if he was a new father. "You're not dreaming."

Kylie laughed. "Billy's the fuckin' pizza delivery boy? Man, this is so cool. Does Steve know?"

"Totally oblivious," Murray lied.

Jason needed reassurance. "He's gonna take us all on and you think Steve won't find out?"

Billy spoke for the first time since they arrived. "You care if he does?"

Kyle was adamant. "Fuck, no. I was only his friend so I could get my cock into you. I'm pretty bored because he won't let me near you."

"What about you, Jason?"

"I'm up for it. I've had sleepless nights dreaming about your butthole."

Billy seemed delighted. "Now I'm all yours. And yours."

He shifted so that his ass was easily accessible and Kyle didn't hesitate to shuck his clothes and had his cock aimed at Billy's pink ass chute before a slightly nervous

Jason had even removed his shoes. I had to admire Kyle's body. He was buff. More buff than me and his cock was just the right length and thickness that Billy enjoyed. I saw him smile as Kyle slid in painlessly. They leaned in to kiss and Kyle was in no hurry to dump a load. Not now that he'd finally managed to nail the ass he'd obviously coveted for years.

While Jason moved closer so Billy could play with his cock, there was another knock at the door and Marty strode in. Marty was a prick. I worked with him. He was straight but I knew he'd always wanted to get into Billy. He tried it whenever my back was turned. He was certainly not on my friends list. Billy must have wanted him here for a reason. Surely not because he wanted his dick up his ass.

"Is that who I think it is?" Marty crowed as Dale handed him a drink. He looked skyward and whispered, "Thank you," before turning to the room and saying, "Now I know there really is a god."

He stripped down to his briefs, his middle-aged body hairy and out of shape. I saw Dale wrinkle his nose in distaste. He sat and watched while Kyle took his time fucking Billy smoothly and deeply. Jason straddled his face and sank his cock between Billy's lips.

Marty absent-mindedly played with his cock through his briefs. "Does Steve know about this little free-fuck-all?"

"It seems not," Kyle called over his shoulder. "Oh, Jesus, this ass is as good as they say. Fuckin' sweet. I could drill him all night."

"Yeah, well, you better hurry up because I want to pop my nuts real bad."

As if on cue, a few minutes later Kyle pushed hard against Billy and screwed up his face. "Ugh. Fuck. Shit. Fuck." It took him a few moments to get his breath back before he pulled out and Billy's fuckhole squelched. Jason had dismounted his face but Marty simply elbowed his way in and had his cock in Billy before Jason even had a chance.

"Hey, Marty, how would you like to fuck me in front of Steve?"

"Any time. I loathe everything that yuppie cunt stands for and would love to take him down. Thinks he's so fuckin' wonderful because he outsells the rest of us two to one."

"You'll tell all his co-workers you fucked me senseless?" Billy asked.

What Marty lacked in finesse he made up for in dogged determination.

"You bet I will. They'll fuckin' laugh at him every time he walks on the floor."

"Make sure you do," Billy said.

"Don't tell me what to do, cunt." Marty spat in Billy's face. It drooled down his cheek to his mouth. Billy poked at it with his tongue, licked it up, and then swallowed it.

"Nasty." Marty gobbed more spit directly into Billy's mouth. "Why don't I take you in the car yard, get everyone to line up and fuck your pretty little ass while Steve watches. Think he'd like that, Billy?"

"Who cares if he likes it?" Billy said.

"Oh, I do, Billy. I care a lot. I'd use you like a lump of fuck meat, show Steve who's boss. Who has the best cock, Billy?"

Billy groaned and I knew he was getting turned on. "You, Marty, you."

"Fuckin' right. Don't you ever forget it!" Marty couldn't seem to fuck and speak at the same time so he clammed up to concentrate on getting his rocks off. He grunted and sweated like an animal and the perspiration dripped into Billy's eyes. Eventually, he muttered "If I'd known how hot your ass is, I woulda thrown you down and fucked you in the street. Now I'm screwing your slutty faithless fuck hole," before letting fly with a string of expletives that made even Dale blush.

As soon as he pulled out, Jason sank into the slimy hole. Three more arrived but Nathan took one look at what was going on and froze. "Does Steve know about this?" he asked. When he was told that I didn't, he turned to Billy and said, "Much as I'd love to fuck you, mate, Steve is my friend. If he'd given permission I'd be up you like a rat up a drainpipe. But," he turned to everyone in the room, "He won't hear it from me." He closed the door as he left. One up for friendship. Not so, Spike, a tattoo punk that I'd befriended when I helped him get finance for a cheap van for his band.

Jason didn't take long to shoot with a barely audible moan and a slight judder of his body. Spike pulled him off Billy and pushed his own prick straight inside.

"So Steve is outa the loop?" he asked as he slammed back and forth, pulling his cock out fully before battering at Billy's sphincter again. I knew from experience it was the most painful way to fuck someone. But Billy was putting up with it. He almost looked as if he was welcoming the pain. Spike was hammering him into the lounge. "You gonna invite Stevie boy over for sloppy sevenths?"

"Would you like that, Spike?" Billy asked.

"Make him watch me nailing you to the floor. Let him see how you should be treated. Let him watch a real cock slam your sexy little body. That turn you on, Billy?"

Billy groaned and Spiked offered him his tattooed bicep. "Like the ink, boy? Worship the ink."

Billy's tongue snaked out and ran over the smooth skin of Spike's arm, and then he buried his nose and mouth in Spike's armpit, sucking and licking noisily, just as the last of the party arrived. Nick and Bryce arrived together and took one look at the well-fucked Billy before they decided they wanted in and shucked their clothes to join the pile on the floor.

"So this is the famed pizza boy everyone is talking about?" Bryce asked.

There was a chorus of agreement.

"Is he as good as the rumors?" Nick queried.

"A million fuckin' times better," Marty said.

"Shit, you'll make me come," Bryce groaned.

"So you all want to fuck Billy in front of Steve?" Dale had Billy's mobile phone in his hand.

A few of them looked startled but there's safety in numbers and they all agreed.

"I phoned him at home earlier this evening but he wasn't there. Let me try him again," Dale had an evil smile on his face.

I realized what he was planning, but I grabbed for my mobile too late, its distinctive ring tone echoing from my hiding place to the astonishment of all but Dale and Murray. With smug superiority Dale flung open the closet door to reveal me holding a cup of coffee in one hand and my hard cock in the other.

After a stunned silence, the laughter began. My humiliation was complete. Dale led me by the cock over to where Spike was still rough fucking Billy.

"Aren't you going to say hello to your boyfriend?" Dale asked.

"Hi, Billy," I muttered.

"Hi, Steve." Billy smiled. "Like what you see?"

Dale squeezed. "If his cock is anything to go by, I think Steve here likes to watch his boyfriend copping it good and hard. Why don't you just settle back and watch the fun, Steve? Who knows, maybe Billy will even let you join in. Or clean out his ass when we've finished."

"Gross," Marty called.

Dale turned to him. "What? You don't like the idea of your slimy cum that's fermenting in Bill's sloppy ass mixing with all ours then finally flushing down Steve's unwilling throat?"

Marty's eyes grew wide. "Now that you put it that way..."

There was no hiding my excitement while I sat and watched Billy fucked by each and every one of them, all declaring they'd never had an ass like it and, naturally enough, wanting seconds.

Billy drew the line at that. "Nah, guys. You got a preview tonight. And I was glad to give it to you. I love you guys fucking me and I can hardly wait to do it again." He went to his vest and took a handful of business cards from the pocket and handed them out. "You want another go then ring the number on the card. The code for what you want is printed on the back. I'll be glad to do anything you want. Anything at all."

The guys started to dress reluctantly.

"You gonna let Steve fuck you?" Marty asked.

"Hell, no. Not after I had the best fucks ever tonight from you guys. That would be an anti-climax. But can you get Steve to help clean me up?"

I could see they would enjoy this. They manhandled me to the floor and lay me down so Billy could squat over my face. Billy pushed his greasy ass cheeks down on to my face and rubbed the slime all over my nose, my forehead and my cheeks. I saw his sphincter strain and a small dribble of cum oozed down over the underside of his balls. Dale held on to my nose so I had to open my mouth. Billy strained again and a large chunk of cum shot out and onto my face. Dale rubbed it in and spooned it into my mouth. The dribble had become a cascade and cum oozed non-stop until I could scarcely keep it all in my mouth.

"Don't you dare swallow it," Billy commanded. "I want to see your best friends' cum all over your tongue. Swirl it around, Steve."

I did as I was told, the slime oozing down the back of my throat. I opened my mouth wide, poking out my tongue. He swapped positions, plugging my mouth with his own, suctioning up all the spooge. While looking down at me, he dribbled the snowball back again, spitting the remnant before he told me to swallow. My stomach heaved as the slime ran down into my gullet, but I kept it down.

I sat in a corner until the visitors left reluctantly and somewhat embarrassed, not knowing how to react to me now that they'd made their intentions clear about Billy. It probably hadn't sunk in as yet that I'd heard everything they'd said. I was sure guilt would set in before lunch tomorrow.

I got dressed quickly. "You want a lift, Billy?"

"Oh, yeah. Just sit in a corner until I finish with these two."

Murray was surprised. "You want more?"

"Sure, didn't I promise you two a turn off the clock?"

Murray stuttered. "Yeah, but I thought—"

"Well, don't," Billy said sharply. "When I say something I mean it. Steve can sit and watch while you two do me again. Maybe he can tell me what a slut I am and how you can fuck my ass until I can't stand up."

As it worked out, that's exactly what happened. I watched my two best friends work Billy over and got to verbally abuse my boyfriend while he cuckolded me, blowing a load in my trousers without even touching myself.

About half an hour later, I followed Billy in the van back to the depot, then he jumped in our car for the drive home. Neither of us spoke about what had just happened and when we got back to the apartment Billy said "Night," and went into his room closing the door. I spent a very restless night, jerking off to the memory of all I'd seen.

****

Billy obviously intended keeping his pizza delivery job because he went out each evening and came back in the early hours of the morning reeking of cum and piss. I tried to speak to him about his behavior but he wouldn't countenance it. I was prepared to allow him certain leeway but fucking the men I considered my friends was beyond acceptable bounds even in my lapse moral code.

I got caught up in the cycle of overtime and mortgage repayments, utility bills and supermarket shopping and my resolve waivered. Billy realized we had to speak some time, and Sunday afternoons, before he headed out to work, became the time that he handed over his wages as I attempted to balance the books. I never queried the small amounts he gave me. He was either on a lousy hourly rate and the tips were not as abundant as he'd expected, men taking advantage of his good nature, or he was salting the money away, perhaps toward a nest egg to leave me and branch out on his own.

On one such Sunday in late November, Billy startled me with a request. "Next Sunday, can you to drive me to Uncle Ram's? It's the company Christmas party. He likes us all to be there."

"What time?"

"Leave mid-morning. To arrive in time for lunch."

Billy had never been close to this side of his family and we had never been invited to share Christmas or any other holiday with them before. Ram owned a house on the south coast at Coalcliff, about ninety minutes from the city, perched on top of a small bluff with its own private beach and a series of rock ledges from which the fishing was plentiful.

"Is the invitation for one or for two?"

"I didn't think you'd be interested," Billy replied. "It will be all my work colleagues. Mainly girls, and a few suppliers. It'll be a bit boring."

"Why are you going then?"

"It's…um…like mandatory. Uncle Ram gives out Christmas bonuses and unless you've got a very good reason for not attending, like death, you don't get it. Plus there are prizes for best delivery girl, best feedback from customers, and all the usual sort of shit."

"The prize being a voucher for one of his own pizzas no doubt." I was thinking of how stingy Billy's wages had been and I couldn't see the bonus or the prizes adding up to much.

Billy shrugged his indifference. "Can you do it? Otherwise I'll have to hire a car to get there."

"What about one of your customers? Dale or Murray could drive you." I regretted saying it the moment the words left my mouth.

Billy sighed. "Uncle Ram doesn't allow fraternization between customers and staff."

"At the Christmas party at any rate," I added.

"Look, forget it. It's no big deal. I'll see if anyone can give me a lift. I only thought it might be a nice change for you. When you're not at work, which seems to be all the time, you're cooped up inside the apartment trying to balance the books..."

I bit my tongue. No use in starting an argument.

"You can go swimming, do a bit of rock fishing, or just relax for the afternoon," Billy continued. "We can drive back when you've had enough. It will do you good."

"You want me to come then?"

"I was afraid you might be bored. If you don't want to, that's your choice, I'll stay overnight, there's no work that night, all the franchises are closed for the party, and hitch a ride back with someone in the morning."

It did sound inviting. I'd been on my guard only because I thought it may have been yet another opportunity for Billy to get himself into situations that would lead to my ultimate humiliation. I didn't think my blood pressure could stand it. The way our relationship was headed, this would be our last Christmas together – if it lasted until then – and I thought we might as well make the most of it. I might even be able to get him drunk and take advantage of him myself. My balls were turning blue from lack of sex. All my overtures to Billy had been rebuffed since he'd begun work at Pizza with Everything.

I couldn't help one last snipe. "Okay, I'll drive you up and drive you back, as long as you don't think I'll cramp your style."

Billy shook his head at my clumsy put down and went to his room, closing the door, emerging only a few hours later to head off to work without even saying goodbye. A few more weeks of this cold shoulder and they'd be locking me up.

The rest of the week passed in much the same way, Billy avoiding me, which wasn't all that difficult given our overlapping work schedules, and me tucking him in and kissing him secretly each morning before heading out, smelling other men's sex on his face and body.

Billy thawed a little by the following weekend, so the scheduled party run was going ahead. Ram was supplying all the food, free beer and soft drinks, plus a fruit punch, and a little home-made grappa which I'd heard was lethal. I packed a half dozen bottles of quality wine to help out, grateful that all gifts, except alcohol, were strictly verboten. Ram would play Santa Claus and distribute small gifts to the children of his employees and the few relatives who still acknowledged his branch of the family tree.

I drove the car out of the underground parking bay and waited for Billy in the street. Okay, we've been together almost six years now, but even I had to whistle when he appeared and hopped into the passenger's seat.

He looked gorgeous. He'd obviously spent a little of his wages on new casual clothes and he certainly knew how to pick garments that brought out his coloring and the beauty of his muscular body and his handsome face. I fell in love with him all over again. He seemed pleased at my reaction and the smile stayed on his face for the next twenty minutes.

I swore to myself I would do and say nothing to spoil the day, no matter the provocation, although I was not expecting much from this family-oriented event. The ninety-minute trip was pleasant, I enjoy driving, although the conversation was sparse. The radio proved a source of irritation and our small talk, we avoided the personal, dried up very quickly, so that for most of the journey Billy listened to his iPod via his ear pieces and gazed silently out the window at the passing scenery.

As the highway wound down the coast we came across spectacular views of the Pacific and the vast expanse of blue ocean lifted my spirits, dulled somewhat by Billy's uncommunicative behavior. When we finally arrived and turned into the driveway of Ram's house, we both were shocked by the opulence. The gravel driveway led up to a two-story white mansion with marble columns pretentiously framing the magnificent carved oak front door. The residence glistened in the hot and humid midday sun, vehicles already clogging the parking spots although I managed to squeeze the car into one of the few remaining spaces. Carrying the box of wine we headed to the door which opened just before we had a chance to ring.

"Billy, glad you could make it. We were just about to send out a search party. How's my favorite nephew?" Ram was a big bear of a man in his late forties, who'd obviously eaten a little too readily of his own product. He was a good 280lbs and stood 6'2". Billy disappeared into his hug. I thought the big man would suffocate him.

He turned his attention to me and almost crushed the bones in my hand he shook it so vehemently. "You must be Steve, we've heard so much about you. Glad to finally meet you. Billy never stops praising your finer points."

I knew he was just being polite but I was surprised to see that Billy had a smut of red in his cheeks.

"Hello, I'm Ruby. Welcome to our family. Glad you could make our little party."

Billy leaned in and kissed her on the cheek. "Hello, Auntie Ruby." She, too, enveloped him in her arms and pressed him to her very large artificially enhanced breasts. Ruby, alias porn royalty Clitty Glitter, whom I had seen gang banged and double penetrated by twelve men in *Orgy on the Orient Express*, was a stunning woman. She still managed the occasional non-sexual guest appearance in hetero porn although it was rumored she was the body double on a number of recent best sellers when the lead actress was unable to accommodate men of, shall we say, extra-large proportions. She also guested as harridan mums and girlfriends in gay porn where she had attracted a cult following.

Her long red hair, her crowning glory and, along with triple penetration, her trademark, was truly spectacular. More impressive yet was the adoring way in which she looked at her husband. This truly was a love match. She hugged me as tightly as she did Billy. She smelled of apricots and popcorn. I liked her immediately and felt right at home.

The wine was taken from me and Ruby walked us out amongst the guests who were already swimming in the pool or else sitting about in groups chatting on the mansion's expansive ground-level entertaining area. A number of young women screamed when they saw Billy, rushing over to claim him, stripping him to his Speedos before dragging him to the pool where they carried on like a bunch of kids.

Ruby took my arm, introducing me to the men, most of whom were the boyfriends of the female pizza delivery crew. I wondered how they coped with their girlfriends' infidelity. The remainder of the guests were cooks and general hands at the pizza franchises, plus a smattering of suppliers. "Billy really is a remarkable young man," Ruby said.

"Yes," I replied non-committally.

She stopped to look at me. "You must be something special the way he talks about you."

"I didn't know he'd been here before," I said.

"Oh, no, he hasn't. I help out in the shop. Sometimes I do the deliveries for old times' sake, when Ram is in one of his shitty moods."

My face must have given me away. "Now, I've shocked you." She laughed and led me along to meet another group of guests.

She left me while she went in to help prepare lunch. I had to admit it was fun standing chatting amiably with a group of strangers not having to worry about Billy. Children raced around screaming, getting tangled amongst the adults, while the beer and wine flowed, as did the bonhomie. I wandered away to look at the superb garden of native plants that had a precarious existence here on the cliff top, buffeted by easterlies that swept in off the salty sea.

I found a sun lounge and sat to watch Billy frolicking in the pool. He waved happily and I saluted him with my drink in acknowledgement. He was the center of attention among the young women, some of whom surreptitiously groped his ass while a few squeezed his cock. He batted them away good naturedly;

otherwise I would have suspected he had bisexual tendencies.

Life was good today. I dreaded to think of our return to the city where Billy would once again take refuge in the spare room. If only he would tell me what the problem was, I was sure we could overcome it.

A shadow obstructed the sun. "You must be Billy's boyfriend."

Shading my eyes I looked up. He was very cute. Mediterranean. Greek, Italian, perhaps Lebanese. He was clothed only in Speedos which did little to disguise the size of his cock.

"Steve." I held out my hand as he sat in the lounge chair beside me.

"Mario. This your first time?"

"Uh huh."

"Your Billy is very popular. And not just here. Natasha...that's her in the red," he said pointing to a stunning blonde who was all over Billy. "She fancies him something fearful. She's tried but she got nowhere."

I smiled. "I think she'll find she lacks the equipment that Billy needs."

"She even offered to wear a strap-on."

I laughed. "That is keen." I looked over at him. "You don't mind?"

He looked serious. "Sometimes. What about you?"

"I was never given a choice."

"Ouch."

We sat and watched the pool. Shortly Ram came out and spoke to Natasha. She got out and dried herself, shaking her wet hair, and waved to Mario before disappearing inside the house.

"What was that all about?" I enquired.

"She was chosen."

"Chosen?"

"Yeah. It's no big deal. The cops turn up throughout the day for their annual pay off. As a special Christmas bonus, Ram lets them choose one of the girls, only the delivery chicks not the wives or anything, for a special in one of the bedrooms. Sometimes they even choose Ruby. It's all very democratic. You can only get chosen once."

He seemed very casual about the process.

"Well, I suppose Billy doesn't have much chance."

"Don't you believe it. Tash tells me he's one of the most popular delivery staff they've ever had. Some of the girls are losing customers to him. Straight guys who want to try it out."

"Like you?"

He chuckled. "How did you know?"

"Easy. That rather lethal looking weapon you've got barely hidden in your Speedos twitches every time you mention his name."

"Why, Steve, are you staring at my cock?"

"If you don't want people to stare at it you shouldn't be wearing those trunks."

"You don't mind, do you?"

"Wouldn't matter if I did. Billy is his own man. But, no, I don't mind. Doesn't mean I wouldn't be as envious as hell. You're a hot fucker."

"You think he'd be interested?"

"With that tantalizing bulge you've got, I think Billy would be bending over in a matter of seconds. I'm surprised you haven't porked him already."

"I never saw him before today. He certainly lives up to all the hype."

"Don't I know it."

"If I get a chance at his ass, Tash wants to watch."

I didn't like her chances.

The lunch went off without a hitch and Billy stayed glued to my side, giving the appearance that we were the happiest couple alive. He was almost like his old self, discussing fantasy partnering, picking out men at the party he'd like to fuck 'if he were single.' I wasn't sure if that qualification about bachelorhood was a threat about the parlous state of our relationship or a confirmation that we were still in one. I didn't dare ask because that was territory he didn't wish to explore at the moment.

He picked out a handful of men who had taken his fantasy, all straight, or so he maintained.

"What about Mario? He's very attractive and seems to have quite a handful down his Speedos."

"I've sort of put him out of my mind because he's Tash's boyfriend," Billy said.

"Hmmm, that never stopped you from fucking my best friends," I pointed out. I knew I shouldn't have said it, but I was still bitter. To cover my faux pas I added quickly, "Besides, it's not like she's exactly faithful. Isn't she fucking for tips when she delivers pizza?"

Billy paused to consider what I'd said. "You think he'd be interested?"

"Definitely. But only if Tash can watch."

Billy grimaced. "Not sure I'm up for that. Particularly as I think she'd probably try to join in at some stage."

Because it was so hot and humid in the garden, most of the guests remained in their swimming costumes, including Billy who was getting more than his share of admiring glances, from men as well as women.

"What's the schedule for this afternoon?" I asked.

"Ram will come out dressed as Santa Claus shortly. He'll give gifts to all the kids who are here then we go through that rigmarole I told you about earlier. He gets the delivery girls to sit on his knee. He gives the prettiest girls a quick feel, nothing too blatant otherwise Ruby would have his balls, he gives them their bonus and they give him a sloppy kiss and then the next one takes a turn.

Before that there's a short ceremony where he hands out prizes for best pizza cook, best pizza delivery, that sort of shit."

"Are you in the running?"

"We all are. It's democratic. Nobody votes or anything. It goes by sales, or workload or the public writing in, that sort of thing. As for me, I don't stand a snowball's. I've only worked there three months. The job is over on Christmas Eve."

"You're giving it away? I thought you liked it?"

"Whatever gave you that idea?" Billy asked.

"I just thought—"

I was saved further embarrassment when Christmas carols blared out over the sound system set up in the barbecue area, and Ram made his appearance dressed in a heat-stroke inducing Santa outfit. Pandemonium broke out as kids squealed and ran to him and his big sack of goodies. Each gift had been especially hand-picked to the taste of the recipient. I was amazed at the trouble to which he'd gone to get things right. Perhaps I had misjudged him.

With the kids safely out of the way and moved to a special part of the garden, under the care of a nanny specifically hired for the occasion to give the parents a respite, Ram got down to the real business of the day. He called for quiet and his workers gathered around him in expectation of cash and the chance at a prize. There was a scattering of applause as names totally unfamiliar to me were called out and prizes awarded. I had to admit Ram was a more generous employer than I had anticipated. Cash prizes were substantial without being ridiculous, but as Billy was eligible in only one category, pizza delivery, and unlikely to win I didn't pay much attention.

Bored guests with no financial or emotional interest in the proceedings drifted off for the afternoon's activities. The men for a booze-up on the beach, the women for a natter and their own space around the pool. There were no hard and fast rules and the sexes could mix if they wished but Ruby told me they kept pretty much to their own domains, until late afternoon when they came together for their farewells.

I joined her in the kitchen to help with the tidy up after the meals. The sound of people slamming their hands down on the wooden furniture and whoops of delight and shrill whistles signaled the event was over. I changed into my swimming togs and headed outside with my beach towel fully intending to take advantage of the sun. I found Billy and he suggested I join the exodus but that he would have to stay until he received his bonus. He looked terribly disappointed so I knew he must have expected to take out one of the prizes. I doubted they had one for the biggest slut or the delivery boy most likely to humiliate his boyfriend.

There was something in the way he suggested I leave, as well as that tell-tale look of guilt when he suggested I would be bored that held me there. I had walked away as if taking Billy's advice but lingered at the back of the crowd out of his view.

The dispensing of Ram's largesse was a tedious and lengthy business. He took pride of place at a large table which had an assortment of envelopes on it. Now that the kids had been shepherded out of sight, he'd removed his Santa outfit except for the boots, his Santa cap and a pair of red shorts. He was a striking looking man, not exactly fat but not exactly buff either. The cooks and general hands were disposed of quickly. A kind word of thanks and encouragement, a quick handshake and an envelope of cash was all it took. It was only when he got to the pizza delivery girls that things got rowdy, and other women made a hasty exit.

The atmosphere got decidedly bawdy, male guests whooping and hollering drunkenly as the girls sat on Ram's knee while he pretended to finger them then sniff and lick his hand, while he made sexist comments about their figures and their loose morals. He was very specific about their expertise in certain sexual proclivities and guests would slap the girl's boyfriend on the back to show their appreciation of her skills. A few of the girls giggled when it was their turn, one shrieked in surprise, and one or two had glazed eyes by the time they got off his lap.

I thought Billy would get a quick hand shake and we'd be on our way. But no, Billy sat on Ram's knee, placing his arms around his uncle's neck to whisper in his ear. There were catcalls and cheers until Ram raised his hands for quiet.

"Billy here, has surprised us all with the amount of business he has generated for the company. Plus the unlimited goodwill. Let's not forget it's his unrelenting hard work that has, in part, been responsible for the larger than usual Christmas bonus you've received this year."

A few of the girls called out their support for Billy, while their boyfriends grumbled.

"So what is it about Billy? Well, we polled our clients, and they tell us it's this." Ram patted Billy's butt cheeks, leaving his big meaty hand there. "So, I thought I'd better inspect the goods myself to see what's so special about it."

A few of the guests squirmed and moved off.

"There's your bonus on the table, Billy. Lean over and get it."

Billy did as he was told and assumed the position. He was bent forward reaching for the envelope when Ram pulled down his Speedos and quickly simulated shoving his fingers into Billy's delectable rear. No wonder he'd wanted me to be absent from this display. I was probably the only person to see the look cloud

Billy's face. This was no simulation, this was real. Ram had his fingers embedded in his nephew's ass. He pulled them free and pushed them into Billy's mouth.

"Hmm," he purred. "Feels so good."

"Why don't you fuck him?" someone yelled from the crowd.

Ram smiled, and it was not a pretty sight. "You think I should."

The chant went up. "Fuck him! Fuck him! Fuck him!"

Ram rubbed his body against Billy's ass and a roar went up. They didn't want reality, they just wanted ritual humiliation.

"Feels so good," Ram said.

"Harder, make him squeal," someone else shouted.

Someone disagreed. "That's sick, man."

In the seconds that people's attention was turned to the naysayer, I saw Ram pull out his cock. Billy's cry of surprise and pain, and the startled look in his eyes, was a dead giveaway, at least to me, that Ram had his cock in Billy's hole. He pretended like he was riding Billy but he was, in reality, up to his balls in his nephew's butt. Gross! Billy really had hit the gutter with an act like this.

As a few of the guests realized this was a real butt fucking, they turned to see if I was in the audience. Billy saw me watching him from the back of the crowd and attempted to push Ram off, but his uncle held him firmly around the waist until he closed his eyes and leaned his head back, his mouth opening, and he shuddered briefly. A few moments later Billy adjusted his swimming costume and headed over to me, leaving his envelope with his uncle for safekeeping.

I made no mention of what I had just seen, and Billy behaved as if nothing untoward had happened, ignoring the fact he had just added illegal activity to immoral behavior.

On the beach proper, a thin strip of sand the size of a pocket handkerchief, the men were playing cricket, so we joined Mario sun bathing on the rock shelf that jutted out into the ocean. We'd seen him from the cliff top, lying in his knee-length black shorts soaking up rays. He was glad of the company and, I suspect, the opportunity to put the moves on Billy.

The two of them kept the conversation going, mainly about comic incidences within the pizza company, something that bored me so I fell asleep. That would also give Mario the opportunity to try his darnedest to win over my boyfriend. It was someone calling Billy's name that woke me from my slumber. Ram's right-hand man had turned up. "Billy, I hate to do it so late in the day, but you've been, um..." he looked at me before going on. "You've been chosen."

"Aw, shit. I'm enjoying myself here. Can't you tell them I've gone home or something?" he pleaded.

"Nah, special request."

"Okay, I'll be right up."

Billy turned to me and, not realizing I knew what being one of the chosen meant, and made his excuses. "Something I've gotta do for Ram. Sorry. But it should only take half an hour or so. I'll be back before you know it."

"That's okay, I'll still be here." I lay back down on my towel.

After Billy had gone, Mario turned to me, "At least he didn't lie."

"He didn't quite tell the truth either," I said. "If you hadn't told me what it meant, I could have spent the afternoon blissfully unaware. As it is now, I have a knot in my stomach."

The party just became a little less relaxing and a great deal more tense.

Mario looked at me. "Sorry. I shouldn't have told you."

"I would have found out."

"I've got an idea," Mario said. "Why don't we go peek at what's happening? If I can't get Billy's ass for real why not watch it in action, second-best thing."

The idea certainly had merit. I wouldn't be exposed as a voyeur, and he wouldn't be fucking with anyone I knew, especially friends of mine, and I do like watching Billy in action. I guess it's a win/win situation.

Besides, my cock was hard as the gravel in the mansion driveway.

Leaving our towels where they were we raced for the stairs. Billy had already disappeared so he would not notice us shadowing him.

"They set a couple of the spare bedrooms aside for these little Christmas bonus bribes and they all have glass doors that open on to a private central courtyard. I know a secret way in. There's plenty of bush and scrub to hide behind so we can watch."

The more I thought about it the more excited I became. No one took any notice of us as we passed the swimming pool going toward the house and we managed to detour down the side passageway without being seen. A high brick wall fenced off the fourth side of the courtyard. I didn't know how we were going to get inside, it was certainly too difficult to scale. The wooden door to the garden was locked and bolted. Checking to see if anyone was watching, Mario carefully manhandled one of the blocks of sandstone that held the door lock in place. It lifted out and the door swung open.

"You sly bastard," I whispered. "You've done this before."

We could hear voices so we propped the door closed before crawling our way across the yard for a better view into the bedroom. The glass doors were open for ventilation in the humid weather, the curtains drawn back to allow what little breeze there was off the sea to infiltrate the room to cool it down. The occupants had no reason to believe they had anything but absolute privacy. The doors to the other rooms were closed and, I assumed, locked. The courtyard was private and there were no upstairs windows on this side of the house. It had been created for secrets.

We found a position where we could sit on the paving stones and look directly into the bedroom.

"Okay, where's the guy I'm supposed to entertain? I want to get this over with and go back to Steve," I heard Billy say. He was seated on the edge of the double bed still in his swimming costume. Ram was pacing.

"Your boyfriend doesn't have a fuckin' clue, does he?" Ram chuckled.

"He's not stupid. He'll catch on quick enough."

"You know you're the most successful pizza delivery...um...person we've ever had. If we could clone you we'd retire millionaires. We have people ringing up begging us to send you over, to be added to the waiting list in case of cancellation. Why would you want to give that up?"

"You wouldn't understand."

"Try me."

"We've had this conversation. I'm not going to change my mind."

"We'll see."

"Okay, if that's what you want to believe." Billy sounded tired. "So where is he?"

"Right here."

"You?"

"Think of it as research. I gotta find out what your secret is so I can repeat it with other guys when you retire."

"Jesus Christ, Ram, you're my uncle. Isn't that illegal?"

"You owe me this much."

"I don't owe you anything. You already fucked me in public. In front of Steve. Okay, so everyone else thought you were kidding around but you and I know the truth." Billy started for the door but Ram grabbed him by the arm and threw him down.

"Holy fuckin' shit," Mario whispered. "What are we going to do?"

"Nothing at all, unless it gets violent," I replied. "Billy can look after himself."

There was no way, even with his muscle development that Billy could overcome Ram's pure brute strength.

"That little quickie outside was just a taste, an entrée. I want the full menu."

"What's to stop me screaming for help?"

"No one will hear you. These rooms are soundproofed."

"What if I accuse you of rape?"

"By the time I've finished with you, you'll be begging for more. No one will believe a slut. Your reputation precedes you."

Ram grabbed Billy by the hair and dragged him to edge of the bed then shucked off his shorts, kicking them aside, his hard cock close to Billy's face.

"What's the big deal, Billy? You've sucked nastier cocks than mine."

"I wasn't related to them."

"I thought that would be an extra bonus, Billy. You take after my side of the family. Look at my cock, boy. Like it?"

Ram was a pretty impressive sight for his age. Naked he was the sort of man Billy loved to dominate him. Big, solid body with a smattering of hair on his chest and stomach and a little on his shoulders, his cock was a long, thick uncircumcised barge pole. The length would not trouble Billy, but the circumference would test both his holes capacity to expand.

"Shit, I think he's going to do it," Mario whispered.

"Of course he's going to do it," I whispered back. "Billy can't resist a cock like that."

Billy looked conflicted. "If only you weren't my uncle."

Ram lifted his nephew's chin up so that they looked each other in the eye. "You can pretend I'm someone else if you want to but it would be a shame to deny yourself the exquisite torture. Don't you feel that sick sensation of excitement in your stomach?"

"I get that whenever I know I'm doing something bad. Or something that will totally humiliate Steve. Like fucking with his best friends."

"It's a powerful aphrodisiac. Embrace it, Billy."

Ram was slowly milking his cock, peeling the foreskin back, rubbing his thumb around the piss slit. Billy was mesmerized.

"It's so nasty. So forbidden. That's why you want to do it. Reach out and touch your uncle's cock, Billy."

Billy wrapped his hand around the hard prick but withdrew it like he'd touched burning coals.

"Take your Speedos off, Billy. Get down on your knees and smell my cock and balls."

Billy did as he was told, sinking naked to his knees to sniff Ram's balls.

"What would Steve want you to do if he was here watching this right now?"

Billy looked up at the mountain of a man towering over him. "He'd want me to worship your cock, Uncle Ram."

Ram reached under the pillow on the bed, retrieving a bottle of poppers hidden there. He uncapped it and took two long snorts before holding it out for Billy to sniff.

"Here, Billy, though I don't think you need it." Billy sniffed like he was vacuuming courage out of the bottle.

Ram capped it and put it on the bedside table within easy reach. It was only a matter of moments before the drug kicked in.

"Come on, nephew, lick under the foreskin. Lick your uncle's hard cock, lick it, that's right, slowly boy, want to make this last. Watching your mouth slide along my shaft...your aunt can suck like a Hoover but she can't give blow jobs for shit, porn star or no porn star. Not like your mouth, Billy."

Billy came up for air. "But she's one of the most famous in the business."

Ram ran his hands through Billy's blond locks. "On screen, Billy, she's a whore; at home, she can be a bit of a puritan. You getting off on this, aren't you, Billy?"

"Fuck, yeah, uncle Ram. I've always wanted to suck your cock, feel it fill my mouth since you used to come over to my dad's place. I used to watch you when you showered. I wanted to go down on my knees and blow you until you dumped in my sweet throat."

"Pity we left it so long then, nephew."

Ram picked up the bottle, handing it to Billy who snorted six times before relinquishing it to Ram who followed suit.

"Open wide, Billy, this will tickle your tonsils."

Ram grabbed the back of his head and began to push his thick cock into Billy's gob. His lips stretched to take it, his eyes watered, he gagged. Ram pulled back a little before pushing it farther and farther toward Billy's throat. I could see Billy regulating his breathing to take it. The amyl had relaxed him and he seemed determined to take it all even if his jaw was dislocated in the process.

"Fuck, your mouth is so warm, nephew. Just a little bit more. That's it, boy. Take it all. Think how proud Steve would be if he saw you swallow your uncle's big, fat prick right down to the root."

That did it! Billy made one last valiant attempt to house the monster. His face was full of cock, his lips straining to take it, his throat raw, his eyes ablaze, and his nose running with a little snot.

"Fuck, nephew, you did it! Not many have ever taken me down to the balls."

Billy had no intention of letting it rest there. He reached for the poppers; slowly taking his mouth off the shaft to rest his jaw, snorted, and then handed the phial to Ram. Once the fumes reached his brain, Billy slammed his mouth over the huge gleaming prick, tickling and squeezing Ram's balls as he pummeled his own face.

"Oh, shit, nephew. Shit. I've never had anyone fuck my cock with their mouth like you're doing." Ram stumbled, almost losing his footing under Billy's oral onslaught and the effects of the amyl. "Suck it, you dirty little cunt," Ram snarled. "Take your uncle's cock right down that slut throat. Want to drown in your uncle's spunk? I bet you do, Billy. Want me to shoot down your throat? All over your face? Leave my uncle spunk in your asshole?"

I eased my prick out of my swimming costume to give it a chance to breathe; it was so hot and hard. I milked it slowly as I watched my boyfriend's debasement at the hands of his uncle.

Billy gagged, spluttered, pulled off and gasped for air before ramming his face down on the slimy cock. Ram held his head and began to take control, he had to be close. Suddenly, he gasped loudly, held Billy's face embedded fully on his prick, and screamed, "Holy fuckin' mother of god."

Billy's throat was bobbing as the sperm shot down into his gullet. He attempted to push Ram off but he was held tight in a headlock. I was afraid for a moment he would pass out but Ram finally released him and Billy sat back on the floor, his breath ragged, his chin a mixture of spunk and puke, his nose running and his eyes filled with the tears of near choking.

"Fuck, that was intense," he managed to gasp.

Ram flopped back on the bed. "Shit, no wonder you were so popular. And if your ass is as half as good as your mouth I'd be tempted to turn for you, Billy."

Compliments always worked. Billy smiled. "Not half as good, Uncle Ram. Twice as good. And I hope you're gonna find out for yourself shortly."

Ram lifted him on to the bed and flipped him on his belly so he could run his hands over Billy's sweet ass. He pressed his fingers at the puckered hole and then moved across the room to get lube from one of the drawers. He passed the bottle of poppers to Billy. "You may need this, unless you've taken a baseball bat up your ass before. I only got half inside earlier. I want my cock balls deep in you this time."

Billy arched his butt making it easier for Ram to pour lube down his crack and massage it into his receptive hole. Billy groaned his appreciation as Ram pushed two fingers inside. Any of his fingers was equal to an average size cock so Billy was being stretched.

"Open me up like this, Uncle Ram, and then flip me on my back. I want to watch your face as you hammer me."

"Good boy. You know, I could get to like this gay shit. Seems to me you're a lot less squeamish than the girls I got on the books. You're game for anything. Maybe I should organize a poker night with some of the boys for you. Without Steve, of course. Think he'd let you out for the night? Of course, you'd be the meat in the sandwich."

"I think Steve might let me, especially if we don't tell him you guys are gonna tag my ass."

Billy knew me too well.

"You opened up enough?"

"Hell, yeah," Billy said, pushing back on to the invading fingers.

"That is one superb ass," Mario said attempting to adjust his cock in his bathers.

Without so much as a 'by your leave', Ram lined up the head of his prodigious weapon against Billy's tiny hole and pushed.

"Holy fuck!" Billy cried. "I can feel every fuckin' inch of that monster."

"You'll get used to it, nephew."

And he did. After a few minutes of Ram plunging his prick in and out of his guts, Billy began to push back to take as much as he could.

"Looks as if you're ready for the hammering of your young life," Ram said, pulling out and flipping Billy over. He pushed Billy's legs up until his knees were against his shoulders. "Boy, you've got no idea how much I've been looking forward to this moment."

Billy raised the bottle to his nose and took a mammoth hit. He threw his head back as the rush hit him. "Fuck my tight little nephew boy cunt, Uncle Ram. Make me scream. Fuck me until I can't stand up."

The rhythm was slow and gentle at first but Billy must have been doing his trick with his ass muscles and Ram uttered little yelps each time he sank his shaft into Billy's chute. He picked up the pace. "You like a bit of uncle cock, Billy? Feels so good knowing you're the son of my cunt brother. Bet he'll shit himself when he hears I fucked his little boy up the ass. Screwed his brains out. Fucked him till he couldn't stand up."

There was something repulsive yet cock hardening watching this guy bend his own nephew over and slam into him. Mario must have thought so, too, as he released his own cock and sighed. "This is so fuckin' intense, man. So sick. So nasty. I gotta jerk off."

Much as I wanted to watch Billy being screwed into the bed, Mario's cock was too good to waste. I shifted my body closer and put my mouth over his drooling prick. He hadn't noticed and gasped when he felt my warm wet tongue. I thought for a moment he might push me away but he took his hand off his shaft and let me go to work while he watched the live action in the bedroom in front of us.

I got only the soundtrack now and it consisted of totally filthy talk with Billy and Ram daring each other in more and more perverse language, more and more depraved fantasies which I'm sure, given half a chance they both would have eagerly enacted. I was pleased to see that I featured heavily in most of them. And, not to be too modest about it, I would have gladly joined in. In fact, I was tempted to stand up and walk into the bedroom now, except for one tiny fact, well not-so-tiny really, Mario's cock.

"You cheap whore, you fuckin' piece of slut meat, feel my cock pounding your asshole, Billy?"

"I want to be your cock whore, Uncle Ram. Feel you bang my nephew cunt."

They were both so sex crazed at the moment I don't think they would have noticed if the world had come to an end.

There was silence except for the sound of two bodies slamming together. Mario groaned softly, "That is so fuckin' gross," and shot his load into my mouth.

I swallowed as quickly as I could and then sat up to see what had caused the outburst. Ram had leaned in to kiss Billy and uncle and nephew were in the throes of the most passionate lip lock I could imagine.

That was enough for Ram to lose it and I saw his body shudder as he shot his cum inside Billy's ass. When they finally separated I saw Billy had shot a load as well as it oozed down his stomach.

They both lay back on the bed exhausted. I thought they may have been embarrassed by what they had done but the first thing Ram said was, "You just gotta come to Christmas dinner here so I can fuck you again."

"I usually go to Steve's parents' place for Christmas but your invitation is much more inviting. Steve can drop me off on his way through."

"He won't mind?"

"Probably, but I want that monster up my butt again as soon as possible."

"Don't forget that poker night."

"That's if Steve lets me."

"Make sure he does. I want to see that look on your face again when I fuck your ass."

Mario and I sneaked back out of the courtyard as they dressed. We headed back to the beach and I gathered up our belongings, returning to the house as Billy emerged from the bedroom. He was happy to leave, he looked flushed and exhausted, and we made our farewells before heading to the car.

We fought all the way home about Billy not coming to my family's usual Christmas celebration and we both said things we later regretted. The chill in our relationship continued right through until Christmas day and, in fact, right up until I dropped him back at Ram's mansion. He didn't bother to say goodbye and I didn't bother giving him his Christmas present. I was so angry I could scarcely drive.

I was about fifty km up the highway when my mobile rang. I pulled over to the side of the road. I thought it was Billy ringing to apologize in which case I would back down as well and offer to come back a day early and pick him up. The caller ID showed that it wasn't.

"Hi, mum. Merry Christmas."

"Merry Christmas, son."

"What's up?" There was a long pause. "Has something happened?"

"No, no. Nothing like that."

"What is it then?"

"I don't quite know how to put this," mum said.

"Come on, spit it out, it can't be that bad."

"Of course not." I heard her take a deep breath. "You are coming alone, aren't you? That slutty boyfriend of yours is not with you, is he?"

I was shocked. "Pardon me?"

"That Billy character. You're not bringing him, are you?"

I could scarcely hold my temper. "No, I told you, he's gone to his uncle's place. I dropped him off about half an hour ago."

"Good. I thought he might change his mind. He was rather rude on the phone."

"Um, when did you speak to him on the phone?"

"Let me see, about two months back, I think it was."

"Who rang whom?"

"I rang him, of course."

"Why?"

"To tell him he was not welcome here."

"Why would you tell him that?"

"I don't want to hurt your feelings, dear. But the boy's a slut. He's proud of it. It's even tattooed on his body. But I don't have to tell you that."

"Apart from the fact the tattoo was forced on him, why didn't you speak to me about this?"

"I thought your silly flirtation with this person would be well and truly over by now. That you would discover for yourself what sort of a person he is and throw him out."

"Just exactly what sort of a person is he, mum?"

"He's a degenerate, Steven. Need you ask?"

"Yes, I need to ask. So you rang and told him he wasn't welcome. What did he say?"

"Not much. He seemed to accept it."

"Did he ask why?"

"He knows why."

"Did he attempt to defend himself?"

"How could he? He said he would abide by my wishes. And then said he would find an excuse to stay away at Christmas. He would not tell you about my phone call because it would upset you. Something about not wanting to make you choose between him and his family, whatever that meant."

"You don't know what that means?"

"Not a clue, dear."

"Precisely where did you get this idea that Billy is a, uh, degenerate."

"Steven, it's really not the time to be discussing this. We can talk further when you arrive."

"No, mum. Now."

"Your father will tell you all about it when you get here. It's quite sickening. It turned my stomach. And your brother, too. How could he be so brazen? They didn't say anything when you both visited to spare your feelings, son."

"So, Billy what? Propositioned dad and Eddie? Is that it?"

"He tried to touch them. Tried to have his way with Eddie in his gym in the basement. And with your father, of all people. Your father was so revolted he wanted to vomit. They don't want to be put in that situation ever again."

"And you believe them?

Of course she did. She had to. Or else acknowledge her marriage was a sham and her son a liar.

She was indignant. "Of course I believe them."

"Is that the same father and brother that came to the city a few months back with their sports team and invited Billy along as their team mascot?"

"They explained that. It was for your sake."

"Okay, I get the picture, mum."

"Good. It's very distasteful. I don't know how your judgment could have been so awry. Let's just forget it and have a happy Christmas dinner."

"Why did you feel you needed to ring me about this now, mum?"

"Your father and your brother didn't want the embarrassment if he turned up unexpectedly."

"I'll bet they didn't."

"It almost sounds like you're taking that man's side."

"You know something, mum. I am. You and dad and Eddie have yourselves a happy little family Christmas because I'm turning the car around and I'm going to spend the day with my family. With Billy. I don't blame you, mum. I'm sorry you got involved. But if I have to take sides, then I'm siding with Billy. Sorry I won't make it home this year. Maybe next. Bye, mum."

I heard her shout, "Steven!" just before I disconnected and switched the phone off. I turned the car around and headed back toward Ram's place. Either destination had been problematic but I knew in which direction my heart lie. I was tempted to speed but I could ill-afford double demerits if I was caught.

It was the longest forty minute drive of my life. Ruby answered the door. "You'll find him down on the rocks." As I raced for the cliff stairs she called, "You'll be staying for lunch?"

"If you'll have me," I called back, hoping she heard me. I could swear I heard her chuckle in response.

I descended to the beach in record time, dreading that I would fall and injure myself in my haste, but I didn't want to waste a second getting to the man I loved. As I trudged through the sand toward the rock ledge I saw him sitting staring out to sea. I crept up and had my arms around him before he was even aware of my presence. I startled him but he didn't turn around.

He hung his head. "I'm sorry."

"So am I."

I held him tightly for what seemed ages without speaking. Finally, he leaned over and picked up the box near him wrapped in Christmas paper. "Merry Christmas," he said, handing it to me. "Go on, open it."

He turned to face me as I tore off the paper to reveal a rectangular box the size of a large envelope. Lifting the lid, I discovered it was full of papers.

"Go on, read them," he prompted.

The first sheet was folded. My heart beat fit to burst as I opened it, dreading it was a letter from Billy saying our relationship was over. Phew! It was a bank statement. I could feel tears welling in my eyes, unless it was his way of telling me he wanted half? I blinked. I had to look again. At first I didn't understand. It was impossible.

"What the fuck, Billy?"

There were far too many zeroes. And the mortgage – it had been paid for the next six months.

"Did you do this?" I asked.

Billy nodded. I threw my arms around him, showering him with kisses.

"I couldn't bear to watch you killing yourself. I had to help any way I could."

"Why didn't you tell me?"

"I couldn't. You wouldn't have approved. I saw how you were when you found out. Especially that night you spied on me with Murray and Dale."

"I wasn't spying. I went there for comfort, I was feeling depressed."

"I know. Dale told me afterwards how they'd tricked you. But I knew you were there. I saw your car in the street as I drove up."

I dug him in the ribs. "Watching you was fuckin' hot, Billy."

"Why do you think I stayed for extra time once I knew you were there? Knowing you're watching me make a slut of myself is the ultimate turn on for me."

"And my so-called friends?"

"I soaked them for every penny I could get. Got them to order more expensive pizzas. That's how it worked. The topping was the giveaway. You could order a plain pizza and I'd deliver it and leave. Or you could order from the Pizza with Everything special menu and that indicated what sort of sexual favors were required. I made sure I was the addictive ingredient so some of your friends, like Marty for example, was having pizza three or four times a week. Some of them are still ringing me believing I'm going to leave you."

"I did, too, when you moved into the spare room."

"I didn't like myself very much. I couldn't let you touch me while I was doing that job. I thought if you touched me it would contaminate us, our relationship. I never wanted that to happen. I had to divorce myself from you to get through it."

I felt ashamed. "Shit, Billy. I didn't make it easy for you."

Billy brightened. "You haven't opened all your present."

I dug back into the box and brought out a cardboard folder. I didn't think I could be any more surprised or delighted. I was wrong.

"Holy fuck!" I realized now why Billy had looked so disappointed at the prize-giving. It was because I wasn't there for the culmination of all his hard work when he was awarded the Employee of the Year accolade. "Is this for real?"

"Two business-class tickets to Rome and an all-expenses paid two weeks in Italy at top hotels, plus $5000 spending money."

I remembered Billy in the bedroom. "What did you have to do to win that?"

Billy winced at my accusation. "Just be the best at my job. It wasn't hard. The girls don't like what they do, whereas I love sex. I know how to flatter men. Plus I had no competition from other delivery boys so I got all the gay orders. I won it fair and square."

I wondered for a moment whether I should actually be congratulating my boyfriend for making me a laughing stock, a cuckold, and fucking every horny male with enough money for a pizza special in the neighborhood. Then I thought of all those Italian men and the moment passed.

"Steve, I need to tell you something. Don't hate me for it."

"I know already, Billy."

"What? How?"

"Mario and I snuck into the courtyard and watched."

"You don't think I'm a sick fuck?"

"Why? Because you did it or because you liked it?"

"Both."

"Well, Mario and I must be sick fucks as well, because we both blew the biggest loads you've ever seen while we watched." Billy got a cheeky grin. "You want to do it with your uncle again, don't you?"

He didn't need to answer.

Billy was puzzled. "What are you doing here? What happened to dinner with the family?"

"My family is here." I wrapped my arms around him more tightly.

"She told you about the phone call?"

"Yep."

"What else did she say?"

"That you were a degenerate. But, hell, she wasn't telling me anything I didn't already know."

Billy took that for the joke I meant it to be.

"And, for my sake, please keep on being a degenerate for as long as you live. Merry Christmas, Billy." I took the very personal gift out of my pocket and handed it to him. It was a small black box. Billy flipped the lid open and his eyes lit up just before he burst into tears. While he was sobbing I took out the gold ring that had inscribed on the inside 100% Pure Slut and slipped it on his finger. I handed him the box and he slipped the one engraved 100% Slut Lover on mine.

Then I pushed him roughly down on the rocks, ripped his Speedos off and fucked the ass off him. It had been too long. Much too long.

FOLLOW STEVE & BILLY IN
BUSTING BILLY'S BUTT

Is voyeurism such a crime – especially if watching your own boyfriend in action with strangers turns you on big time?

Steve and Billy's monogamous relationship has gone stale until Billy, ever the exhibitionist, shows them a way to spice up their sex life.

Billy has the most coveted ass in the city and Steve loves to watch him secretly spread it open for strangers. But can their relationship survive when Billy goes too far and offers himself to Steve's worst enemies.

YOU MAY ALSO LIKE JAZMIN STARR'S GAY DICKS FOR STRAIGHT CHICKS

What makes gay men so attractive to straight women?

It's a story as old as time itself: hot gay guys are great in bed, have good grooming, gym-toned bods and are as handsome as fuck. All they need is a bad woman to show them the joys of the 'other' side. The conversion may not be permanent, it may last no more than a night but oh, what a night! In some cases it may just be the experience they need to explore their bi side.

It may not be an instruction manual, but it just might give you a few ideas.

ABOUT THE AUTHORS

Barry Lowe writes about love and sex so he won't forget how to do it. When he's not scribbling his adventures for the Sydney gay weekly SX, or out doing field research, he's writing about love's wonderful variations for a series of smut eBooks, novels and anthologies for Lydian Press

 Go to www.barrylowe.info

Jazmin loves sex. It's a serotonin booster, it's cheaper than a loaf of bread, and nowhere near as fattening unless you're doing it with chocolate sauce or whipped cream. The only thing better than the real thing is writing about it.

She loves sex in all its myriad forms. Sometimes she even mixes a little romance with the sex although she thinks vanilla is only for ice cream.

jazminstarrwriter.wordpress.com

OTHER WORKS BY BARRY LOWE

NOVELS & ANTHOLOGIES
Available in eBook and Print

BUSTING BILLY'S BUTT: A Gay Erotic Romance
Steve and Billy's monogamous relationship has gone stale until Billy, ever the exhibitionist, shows them a way to spice up their sex life.

THE MAJOR AND THE MINERS: A Gay Historical Romance
1930s Australia: Two men from opposite ends of the social spectrum. Is love enough to overcome the obstacles between them?

THE GRAVY TRAIN: A Murder Mystery with Recipes
Someone on the train has an appetite for murder!

A TOUCH OF THE SON: A Gay Novel
Their secret passion will lead them to hell. Will they be able to find their way back?

ROMANCING THE BONE: Gay Romance Erotica

OMG! NOT ANOTHER GAY EROTICA ANTHOLOGY?

ROUGH & READY: Gay Tough Guy Erotica

YOUR BOYFRIEND IS HOT: Gay Cuckold Erotica

BEAR SKIN: Hot Gay Bear Erotica

THE MORE THE MERRIER: Gay Gangbang Erotica

THE BOY IS A BOTTOM: Gay Anal Erotica

COCK-EYED OPTIMISTS: Gay Romance Erotica

BABY, I'M NOT A MONSTER: Gay Vampire and Other Paranormal Erotica

SELECTED SHORT FICTION
Available as eBooks

TUNNEL VISION

HARD ON HIS HEELS

SPIN THE BOTTOM

THE NEW DAD'S CLUB

FOUR ON THE FLOOR

TAGGED BY THE TEAM

WANNA SHARE YOUR HUSBAND

For all Barry's titles please visit his page at:
www.lydianpress.com

OTHER TITLES BY JAZMIN STARR

Bobby's Girl
Cops & Throbbers
Great Balls of Fire
Gay Dicks For Straight Chicks

Please visit Jazmin's page at www.lydianpress.com

Lydian Press is dedicated to bringing you the
finest GLBTQ erotic literature on the web.

Visit us on the web at:

http://lydianpress.com